CHRISTMAS IN PRETTY BEACH

POLLY BABBINGTON

COPYRIGHT

AuthorPollyBabbington.com

Want more from Polly's world? For sneak peeks into new settings, early chapters, and bits and bobs from Polly's writing days, sign up for Babbington Letters.

1

Wrapped in a gigantic, very soft, grey cashmere scarf with little bobbles on the end, Sallie Broadchurch walked along the laneway right in the centre of Pretty Beach. The little town by the sea was behaving itself and showing off to the max. It had always liked to think it was special and, approaching Christmas, it ramped things up a bit. Was Pretty Beach going for festive season gold? It most surely was. It was so sparkly, so twinkly, so glittery, it could certainly win a medal for its efforts. The town and its inhabitants were absolutely no strangers to blowing one's own trumpet, and at Christmas, they went for their lives. For sure, Pretty Beach loved to bask in sunshine through the summer months, it embraced all things cosy in the autumn, and loved spring in all its glory, but it really went overboard with loveliness at Christmas time. Christmas in Pretty Beach? There for it. Every single year, sign me up and throw tinsel at my head.

As Sallie ambled along, taking in the glorious sight of the town dressed in its festive finery, she smiled. Every lamppost was dressed with a twirl of tartan, fairy lights twinkled from just about anywhere that didn't move, and the whole place was blanketed in the most gorgeous dusting of soft, twinkly, white snow. Just like a scene from the front of a Christmas card that had been doused in actual glitter, Pretty Beach ring-a-ding sparkled. Sallie couldn't quite get enough of it as she dawdled along the laneway, taking in shop windows here and there. Oohing and ahhing as she looked at the decorations and the white stuff all around, she vacuumed it up. A little commentary ran through her head as she revelled in the decorations and festive feel. *Try and be cool about it, Sal. You're a fully grown woman with a baby and a carol service to run, not a five-year-old who's just seen a snow globe come to life.* But honestly, anyone who knew Sallie Broadchurch knew how much she adored snow and when it dropped on Pretty Beach in December, it gave her all the feels.

The snow had arrived early and heavier than promised, belting the lanterns along the laneway, covering the bunting and laying itself over roofs and the lighthouse in a thick blanket of white. Pretty, yes, absolutely. Helpful, when you had a Christmas carol service to run, a business to keep afloat and a baby to look after, not especially. Sallie checked one of the many lists in her head regarding her upcoming event, a carol service at her property, The Orangery in Pretty Beach, which she'd been planning for months. Everything was planned, thought through and organised, but there was nothing that could be prepared or done about the weather. She'd prayed for a light dusting of snow and the weather gods had certainly fulfilled her wishes. It's just that it was beginning to look as if they'd taken her brief a little bit too literally. When she'd first seen the weather app forecasting snowfall, she'd danced in the kitchen, but it had just kept on coming and showed no signs of letting up. Now she was concerned.

When she'd started to fret that the snow could potentially be a problem for the event, her husband Ben had kept on saying it didn't matter because the carol service didn't have to be perfect. Technically, of course, he wasn't wrong, but Sallie Broadchurch liked perfect, so very perfect. It was easy for Ben to say being perfect was overrated, but Sallie ran with and relied on the well-deserved reputation that her events were the best on the coast, and she wasn't about to let that change anytime soon. Looking up at the heavy snowfall settled on the tops of the higgledy piggledy chimney pots of Pretty Beach, she swallowed and hoped that the weather would behave itself until the first carol was sung. That way, she could have her cake and eat it. Never a bad thing.

Walking along the pavement with her mind full of the logistics of the carol service, she held her face up as soft flurries of snowflakes caught in the breeze coming in from the sea. For a minute or two, she stood and watched as the huge town Christmas tree sparkled in a plethora of white lights. Inhaling, she nodded. Pretty Beach even managed to get the festive smell right; woodsmoke, the sea and pine all rolled into one. A small gathering of locals with bobble hats and mittened hands stood around the door to the bakery chatting, and a gigantic sparkly white reindeer on the bakery roof looked down from above. Fairy lights looped from window to window, crisscrossed across the laneway, swaying in the sea breeze, and little lanterns lined up in doorways twinkled as if their life depended on it. With beautiful snowflakes fluttering down on the scene, Pretty Beach had never lived up to its name more. Sallie Broadchurch couldn't get enough. Really, nobody could.

Pausing for a second outside Maisy's café, Sallie peeked through the steamed-up glass and smiled. Inside, it was packed with locals crammed at the tables, mince pies were loaded behind the counter, and, as the door opened, a scent of Christmas spices, pine and orange spilt out onto the street. Sallie nodded and squinted past in the direction of the lighthouse. If only she could bottle the sound, the smell and the feeling of the place and send it to every little town on the planet: one sniff and world peace would be achieved.

Despite her nerves about the carol service and thoroughly enjoying herself, Sallie made her way in the direction of the bakery. The laneway glowed as if it had been dipped in fairy dust, and snow-covered bunting caught in the breeze. Snowflakes drifted down in spirals, and, laughing to herself, she stuck out her tongue and waited for one to land. If there was one thing she loved, it was snow and all that came with it. In fact, every year, she couldn't quite wait for the white stuff to arrive. Every single December, she sent up a prayer for snow, and each year, so far, the town had delivered. Truth be told, Pretty Beach *always* delivered. Winter wasn't any different and for its snowfalls, it got gold stars all around.

On the air, Silent Night drifted in waves along the laneway, and the smell of the bakery's special Locals Only Christmas cinnamon buns mingled with the coastal smell of Pretty Beach. Arriving at the bakery door, Sallie wasn't surprised to see a queue inside winding all the way around the shop. In fact, it looked as if half the town was picking up their festive orders. Pushing open the door, a bell tinkled overhead, Christmas carols played, little candles in votive holders were set up on every available surface, and each of Holly's staff was dressed in red Christmas outfits. Of course they were.

Holly was adorned in sparkles most of the year, and at Christmas, she made the most of the season. Unofficial mayoress or indeed Queen of Pretty Beach and very successful bakery owner, she not only sparkled with her usual diamonds, no, for Christmas, she took the glitter memo up a notch. You didn't need to look too closely to see that Holly was, in actual fact, powered by batteries. In high-heeled glittery shoes, sparkly tights and a white tutu lit by tiny white lights, she twinkled from head to toe. A halo glittered on top of her head, diamonds sparkled at her ears and on the sides of her cheeks, little glitter flourishes caught the light. Holly, it had to be said, was in her element. She positively radiated Christmas from every pore.

'Sal! Where's Baby Loulou? Ooh, look at you all rugged up. You won't need that scarf on in here. We might as well be open-roasting chestnuts, it's that hot.'

Xian, Holly's mum, followed behind in a fluffy Christmas jumper and sliders topped with Christmas tree clips. With a glittering headband and lit-up Christmas trees dangling from her ears, Xian held out a gigantic tray of hot chocolate in little white paper cups. 'Hey, Sallie! How are you? Where's Loulou?'

'She's with Ben and no doubt she's in charge. She runs our household.' Sallie chuckled as she unwound her scarf and tucked it into her bag. 'I had exactly one hour to myself, and I'm using every second of it.' Internally, Sallie was exponentially pleased with her sixty minutes of peace. Not that she didn't adore her darling baby daughter, Loulou, but having some time to wander around Pretty Beach at Christmas, take it all in and revel in the snow was worth its weight in gold.

Holly gasped, pressed one hand to her sparkly chest and joked. 'Sixty whole minutes? What a luxury! What have you done with *all* that time to yourself?'

'I have been soaking in Christmas from every single corner of our little town. Honestly, the sprinkling of white has made everything look so lovely. As if this town needed anything to make it look better. I love snow.' Sallie didn't add that she was actually rather nervous that the snow might affect the carol service if it continued to fall at the same rate. No one needed to know her concerns. She'd keep them locked up inside in a little box whilst on the outside she pretended everything was tickety-boo.

Holly agreed. 'Living the dream, are we not? Me too, I love snow.' Cackling, Holly flourished her hand in the direction of her mum. 'There's not too much of the white stuff where we're originally from. We've loved snow and chilly weather here right from the word go.'

Sallie shook her head. 'It's so festive everywhere. I've been past every shop and chatted here and there, and everyone is so in the Christmas spirit.'

Holly nodded. 'I did my rounds earlier. Yes, it's buzzing and lots of people are talking about the event at The Orangery. Our town folk love a few carols, do they not?'

'We're all here for it,' Xian whooped. 'No pressure or anything.'

Sallie shook her head. 'Don't scare me.' *As if I need any further pressure. Heart rate is currently doing the conga.*

'You would go and do it to yourself. You're livestreaming one of your events to the world via Lucian's podcast. Good luck and crossed fingers will be needed for everything to go well, especially with the weather forecast. I will pray for you and us.' Xian laughed.

Lucian, an acquaintance of Sallie, was the owner of a podcast, Where the Heck is Pretty Beach? It had started as a tiny podcast with a handful of listeners, which had grown to a global media company. The podcast had helped Sallie's business get established in the early days and she was well aware of its impact. Her carol service was an integral part of Lucian's company's Christmas festivities programming, with a lot resting on its success. Sallie shook her head and swallowed. 'I must be bonkers to be doing it.'

'You are!' Xian offered Sallie a hot chocolate from her tray. 'You look like you need one of these, or maybe a hot toddy from out the back. Locals Only, of course. I made it myself. It has a few extra nips of my Special Drink in it, but keep that to yourself. Fancy one?'

There was no way Sallie was brave enough to down one of Xian's concoctions. 'Tempting, but no, thanks.' She accepted a hot chocolate gratefully and sipped. The chocolate, thick and rich, topped with whipped cream, a dusting of cinnamon and sprinkles of gold edible glitter, tasted like Christmas in a cup. 'This is lovely.

You're both angels.' Internally, Sallie felt as if she needed more than a bit of whipped cream to help her. With the upcoming carol service, weather forecast and two seasonal weddings before Christmas, she needed liquid bravery with sprinkles on top.

'Yep, we are angels sent from above.' Holly chuckled and flicked her lit-up tutu so it swished. 'Now, let's get you sorted. Your order's already boxed up behind the counter. I put in extra because I know how many events you've got on. Your catering order will arrive directly at The Orangery for the carol service as discussed. How's The Orangery looking, by the way? I heard Lucian's been there since dawn, setting up cameras and whatnot.'

'He has,' Sallie confirmed, taking another sip of the hot chocolate and sighing with pleasure. 'He's determined to make it go viral, which is lovely but also terrifying. What if we mess it up? What if the choir goes off-key or someone trips over a cable, or I don't know? I've thought about everything that can possibly go wrong. I should be used to it by now, but this is a *big* deal. That podcast has a lot of clout.'

Holly nodded. 'It has. We always see more website visitors every time an episode goes out.'

It wasn't an exaggeration to say that Sallie had gone over everything that could go wrong. Lucian had told her casually that the service would stream around the world, as if it were completely run-of-the-mill. To him, to be fair, it was. Since then, she had been rehearsing emergency backup plans in her head at three a.m. She'd thought about everything from microphones to the snow to her outfit and had lists of lists and plans of plans.

'Don't even think about what might go wrong,' Holly commanded, swirling glittery fingernails around. 'The Orangery is going to be magical because you're in charge and Suntanned Pete and Lucian are involved. Plus, you have the queen of Christmas herself, Juliette Sparkles, doing her thing. End of story. You don't need to worry.'

Sallie nodded, but inside she was *extremely* nervous. The carol service at The Orangery had somehow become Pretty Beach's main Christmas attraction and very much part of the town's festive calendar. The whole place was counting on it being perfect and this year Lucian was livestreaming it to hundreds of thousands of people. No pressure then.

She was prepared but felt as if she were running on three hours of sleep and fumes. Laughing to herself, she thought about how her life was now so full. When she'd first arrived in Pretty Beach with not much more than a suitcase and backpack, she'd wanted a new start and a cosy little life by the sea. She'd, in fact, got a baby, a town that sparkled on cue, a thriving small business, and now, this year, an event that was likely going to be seen around the world. *Breathe. Shoulders down. One foot in front of the other. And maybe one of Xian's concoctions to sip on the run.*

Once back on the laneway heading home, Sallie glanced down the street and felt butterflies swoop in her stomach. The carol service loomed and every minute mattered. She'd promised herself it would run perfectly. The Orangery would glow, the choir would sing, and there would be no one stuck in the snow. However, as she stood on the pavement and watched snow falling nineteen to the dozen, she knew through experience that they would be lucky for it to go without a hitch. Best laid plans.

Attempting to breathe and not worry, Sallie tried to tell herself that she was ready for anything. But there was a lot riding on her success, at least in her head. As she'd been juggling work, Loulou, and the endless Pretty Beach calendar, she'd sworn the event would prove she could do it all; run a business, be a lovely mummy to Loulou, and have a wonderful Christmas with Ben. Would she be able to pull it all off? Time would tell.

Whatever happened, Sallie would not let herself fail. There was no room for failure in her life. That she knew for free.

2

Further strolling along the laneway and engaging in a fair old bit of dawdling at Christmas lights in festively dressed windows, Sallie turned onto Strawberry Hill and let out a little sigh of pleasure. Quite how she'd ended up living in the street was beyond her, but there was no doubt she adored it. At Christmas, it was dressed up to the nines and even more glorious than at other times of the year. Stopping for a minute, she let her eyes wander up and down the tree-lined road: intricately designed porches draped in gold baubles, white lights in trees, black wrought-iron fences entwined with twinkles, huge stars on double-width front doors. The street wasn't only aesthetically pleasing, nope, it housed a lovely assortment of neighbours, mostly true-blue Pretty Beach peeps who'd lived in the little town by the sea their whole lives. Sallie still had pinch-me moments regularly when walking home up Strawberry Hill. She'd certainly been in worse places in her life: being left with absolutely nothing by the horror of an ex-husband sprang to mind. That, though, was far, far, far in the past. Our girl Sallie was living the dream.

Walking up the path to her house, she nodded to herself as

she looked up. Not bad, not bad at all. Very nice, in fact. The door wore a huge fir and eucalyptus wreath wrapped in tiny white lights, lanterns sat on either side of the entrance mat, and a stack of wood for the woodburner added to the scene. Through the window, a floor-to-ceiling tree that had, let's just say, been an investment, sparkled from its head to its toes. Dressed in thousands and thousands of cluster lights, it was doing an excellent job of fulfilling all Sallie's long-lusted-after festive dreams. This was not a place for chilli pepper-shaped coloured lights, not at all.

Opening the door, Sallie slipped her boots off on the mat, hung her coat in the cloakroom and glanced through into the sitting room at the tree. Chuckling to herself, she nodded. The tree and its cost had been a decision and a half and one she'd mulled over for far too long. Now standing in situ, it was more than worth all the deliberation. She just needed to make sure she hid the receipt. No one needed to know how much the tree had released from her bank account.

Assuming that Loulou might be asleep, she tiptoed into the kitchen and again nodded as she stepped in. Simple, twinkly, festive and so very warm and cosy. When she'd first viewed the house, it had been the kitchen that had sold Sallie hook, line and sinker. She'd known at the time its potential. Now, what she'd seen on the first viewing looked back at her in droves, just a million times better and its transformation still made her catch her breath. The kitchen, the house on Strawberry Hill and her business were Sallie's philosophy on life all over; proof that hard work, dogged effort and stubbornness counted for something. A lot of elbow grease, gritted teeth and a decent paintbrush were part of the equation, too. Roll up your sleeves and get the devil on with it had been Sallie's mantra her whole life, and oh, how standing in a Strawberry Hill kitchen did that hard work look back at her in droves.

For a moment, she stood and basked in the glow of all her

own hard work. The Aga had been restored to its full glory and presided over the room like a queen. Sallie had found a specialist restorer who'd nearly wept with joy when he'd seen it. 'They don't make them like this any more,' he'd said. Sallie had thought that he'd been right to cry and had joined in when he'd finished.

A ten-seater mahogany table that she and Ben had purchased with the house had also gone through a major transformation and now sat happily doing its thing. Once upon a time, dusty, underloved and groaning under piles of detritus, now white-washed to a soft, chalky finish, it sent out an invitation to sit down with a cup of tea. Around it, mismatched café chairs in cream and white begged to be sat on, and a festive fir, pine, and eucalyptus runner ran down the centre. Interspersed with cream pillar candles, sprigs of holly, and tiny gold baubles that caught the light, for Christmas, the table twinkled. The brief in Sallie's head for the table had been that it would be the centre of the old house on Strawberry Hill. A place to collapse at the end of the day, somewhere to chat and have a cup of tea, a space to hold casual suppers, have friends over, house a laptop or two. The old table full of love, looking back at her, fulfilled the brief beautifully.

Everything about the kitchen made Sallie's heart sing. Shelving around the top was filled with her collection of cream stoneware and vintage ironstone, old copper moulds hung from hooks, and here and there, pieces of blue and white transfer-ware added pops of colour. Linen Roman blinds in the softest oatmeal-cream hung at the window, garlands of fresh festive greenery were draped along the top of the cupboards, white Christmas lights twinkled, and a wooden Advent calendar with tiny drawers hung on one wall.

Hearing Ben cross the hallway, Sallie turned as he opened the door with the monitor for Loulou in his arms. Ben smiled. 'All good?'

'Yep. Is Loulou still asleep?'

'Yes, she is for now.'

Sallie hoped that fact would be true for another twenty minutes. 'Ahh, she must have slept a while.'

'She went out like a light. How was the town?'

'Good. The snow makes everything look so festive.'

Ben looked out the window. 'It's still coming down fairly hard.'

Sallie raised her eyebrows. 'I did pray for it.'

'You did. Tea?' Ben walked towards the kettle as Sallie put down the white bag from the bakery.

'I'd love one. I was just thinking about how different it all looks in here and, wow, how far we've come since we bought the place. What a mess it was when we moved in. Do you remember how crazy it was in this room?'

Ben shuddered. 'I'd rather not. It's been a journey and a half.'

Sallie laughed to herself at the "journey" word; Ben's polite code for the chaos they'd lived with when they'd first moved in. Chaos with a happy ending, certainly, but chaos all the same. She leaned back against the worktop as the Christmas lights sparkled, the Aga hummed, and the fir garlands twinkled overhead. 'What do you reckon the people who lived here before would think about it now?'

'I don't think they'd think it was the same house.' The baby monitor crackled and they both held their breath. Ben whispered, 'She's been down for a while. I'm calling it a Christmas miracle.'

'We'd better make the most of it. Do not tempt fate.'

Ben chuckled. 'I think she's part alarm clock. How come she's so small yet she rules this roost?'

Sallie laughed and joked. 'She has standards and takes after her father. I am merely staff around her.'

Ben poured the tea. 'What did they say in the bakery? I bet it was heaving in there. There's usually a queue well managed by Holly and Xian at this time of year.'

'Yep, it went all the way around the inside of the shop. Holly looked like a walking Christmas tree and Xian was giving out hot chocolate willy-nilly. She offered me one of her Special Drink concoctions, which I obviously declined. There was a lot of talk about the carol service.'

'And?'

Sallie made a wincing face and nodded in the direction of the window. 'I don't know. I have to say I'm concerned because of the adverse weather.' Sallie didn't totally voice her honest thoughts that she'd been awake worrying that things would go pear-shaped. She was bracing herself because it mattered to her *a lot.*

'It'll be fine. You've been planning this for months and everything's organised. Lucian's got backup plans for the backup plans, and even if something does go wrong, it'll still be magical because you made it and it's in Pretty Beach. That's what this town does; it makes magic. Plus, Suntanned Pete is involved, so whatever happens, he'll be there to save the day. We all know that.'

'I know. So many things can go wrong at these events, though.'

'Your most important asset is that you have me available to assist and I make everything better.' Ben was straight-faced as he joked.

'In your dreams.'

'Oh, come on. I'm a catch and don't you know it.'

Sallie laughed as she looked out the window. *Oh, she knew it for sure.* There was little to no doubt about that. Ben was handsome, nice, kind and very, very, *very* rich. Not that she cared about the latter, of course not. Snow fell past the glass and settled on the lawn. 'I'm not disputing that *you're* a catch. I'm just a better catch than you.'

Ben bantered back. 'I'll remind you of that when you're busy and I'm annoying you.'

'Ha.'

Ben looked out the window. 'Everything is turning whiter by the minute.'

'I do love snow, though. It makes everything so calm and pretty, doesn't it? I even like the sound. It sort of muffles everything, doesn't it?'

'Yeah, but you are *weird* about it, Sal. You're a person who prays for snow from about September onwards.'

'Guilty. I've always been the same. We don't want much more, though, otherwise there's going to be drama with people getting to The Orangery.'

Ben leant over the sink and peered further out into the back garden. 'It needs to stay like this.'

'Once the carol service is over, it can snow as hard as it likes. Actually, I wouldn't even mind if we got snowed in for Christmas.'

Ben contemplated and nodded. 'That sounds quite attractive. It would just be us and Loulou. It's been a busy year.'

'You can say that again.'

'You've had so much on your plate this year. Thank God, it's nearly winding down time. Next year, I am telling you now, you're taking it easy...'

Sallie couldn't argue with that. She *had* been busy. She felt as if she'd stumbled through most of the year in a state of permanent exhaustion and mild panic. Having Loulou had completely changed her world. Somewhere underneath, she was still the same old Sallie, but maybe it was time to admit that she couldn't do everything all the time. Swallowing, she hoped she'd get through the carol service and her last two weddings of the year unscathed. Then it would be Christmas and she would be able to let her hair down and enjoy the festive season. For now, she just had to get through one thing at a time. Hopefully, she'd make it through without any issues. Probably a good idea if she didn't hold her breath.

3

With Loulou fast asleep in the pram, Sallie walked into Maisy's, a coffee shop in Pretty Beach, more than ready for a catch-up with her best friend Nina. Sallie had known Nina for years and after Sallie had moved to Pretty Beach and loved it, Nina had also relocated to the town. Now, both Sallie and Nina had been infiltrated into the funny little ways of Pretty Beach and had adopted them with gusto.

Sallie had been up since the crack of dawn. Early that morning, she'd left Loulou with Ben and had been to The Orangery to finish the last few arrangements for the carol service. She'd then returned home to swap reins with Ben, visited her other business venue to resolve an internet issue, and was now hoping to have five minutes to sit down with a cup of tea. In other words, she had a lot going on.

It had to be said that our lovely Sallie was a little bit frazzled. Mostly because of the carol service preparations, but also the time of year. In addition, she was tired after a busy summer wedding season at The Orangery, and she still had two large festive weddings to go. It was the carol service, however, that was her main headache and was getting very near to tipping her over the edge. The service had become a very favoured and integral part of the town's festive calendar, with the bar for it to succeed exponentially high. Sallie did not take it lightly and was feeling it every which way. Not that she let anyone know that, of course not. She felt lucky enough to have been well and truly welcomed into the inner circles of Pretty Beach and therefore did not want to let anyone down. There would be no ball dropping in Sallie's world. Just a whole lot of trying to keep everything up in the air.

Maisy's was buzzing with locals and festively dressed for the occasion. Garlands of pine looped from the ceiling, miniature trees in terracotta pots sat on every table, and carols played from hidden speakers. Crossing her fingers that Loulou would stay asleep, Sallie smiled and waved at Nina on the far side of the room. After ordering a Locals Only hot chocolate, she manoeuvred the pram to the table, tucked it in the corner out of the way and pulled down the hood. Loulou had been a little angel all morning and was now ensconced in the delights of the Land of Nod. Sallie wanted thirty quiet minutes, a hot drink at a civilised temperature and some adult conversation.

Xian, from the bakery with sparkly reindeer earrings dangling from her ears, was sitting at a table adjacent to Nina. She looked up from her iPad, pointed to the pram and whispered, 'Fast asleep?'

'Yes, and hopefully staying that way for a bit,' Sallie whispered back with a smile. 'How are you?'

Xian pointed to her iPad. 'In the middle of a deal in Singapore.'

Nodding, Sallie slid into the chair opposite Nina with a long exhale. Nina, as usual, looked put together, confident, and as if she had all her ducks in a row. With a camel coat draped in a perfect fold over the back of her chair, a silk scarf tucked around her neck and her hair sleek, she smiled. In front of her sat a flat white with a little biscotti perched on the side. *Of course she looks like that,* Sallie thought to herself. It had been the same for as long as Sallie had known Nina. Nina never had a hair out of place. Clearly, a skill she'd been born with, and one Sallie often mused. *Neat scarf, neat coffee, neat life.*

Nina beamed. 'Hiya. How are you? Did Loulou sleep through last night?'

'She did. She's been a darling. We've tag-teamed with her this morning. She's so sweet.' Sallie glanced into the pram.

'Aww, she is.'

'How are you?'

'Yeah, fine.' Nina narrowed her eyes. 'You're not looking yourself. You've got that stressed look. Do you need help with anything?'

Sallie laughed and waved her hand in dismissal in front of her face. 'I'm fine. I'm just trying to make sure everything runs smoothly.'

Nina stirred her coffee. 'Which is code in your language for not allowing a single snowflake out of place. Am I right?'

'Well, it *is* The Orangery and I *do* want it to be perfect.' Sallie scanned the pram as Loulou gave a tiny murmur, and she froze.

'How did you get on this morning?'

'I didn't have a lot of time. I did everything by the skin of my teeth, but yeah, there's nothing more I can do now apart from the things that need to be done on the day. Oh, and pray we don't get a blizzard.' Sallie put her gloves in her bag and started to pick marshmallows off the top of her chocolate.

'You seem to be stretched really thin at the moment,' Nina observed.

'I am. You know me. I *love* being busy. Who wants to sit around twiddling their thumbs all day?'

'No one but people have a limit.'

'I'm fine.' Sallie sipped her drink.

'You always say that.'

'I'm just busy.' Sallie stirred her chocolate. 'Ahh, I just needed a sit down, a nice warm drink and Loulou to have a snooze for a bit. If she wakes up, we'll know about it.' *And so will everyone else within a three-street radius.*

Nina stood up and peeked into the pram. 'She's perfect, Sal. What a darling.'

'Yep. She certainly makes life busy!'

Nina shook her head. 'Honestly, I don't know how you do it all. The Orangery, the baby, the house, all the weddings and events you've done in the last few months, and you still turn up to coffee looking half decent. I'd be in bits.'

Sallie snorted and joked. 'Rubbish! Says the woman who held down a full-on job through the newborn stage and made leisure wear look attractive.'

Nina raised her eyebrows. 'On the outside, maybe. You're not fooling me. I know how hard it is to run a business and have a baby. It's not for the weak and you're doing a lot.'

'I'm fine. I'm holding myself together with caffeine and Christmas-shaped cinnamon buns.' Taking a sip of the hot chocolate, Sallie closed her eyes for a moment. *Bliss.*

'So, everything is on schedule for the carol service?'

'I think so.' Sallie internally rolled her eyes. *Think was one part of it, hope the rest.*

'What about from Lucian's end?'

'He's all over it. It's his business and his livelihood, so he's good at it. There are people tuning in from all over the show. He has followers from around the world. From Tokyo to Toronto, people will be watching. Can you believe that? Pretty Beach goes global.' Sallie laughed and gulped. It sounded wonderful in theory, nausea-inducing in practice.

Nina nodded. 'He's worked so hard to get that podcast to take off. Funny, really, when you think about it. Technology is amazing. It connects people from all parts of the world at the speed of lightning.'

Sallie shuddered. 'And don't I know it. If one fairy light

blows, the whole world will see it. Imagine the comments. Actually, no, don't. It doesn't bear thinking about.'

Nina shook her head. 'You've done all the work. Now you just let the town do what it does best.'

Sallie nodded. It was easy for Nina to say. As ever, Nina looked immaculate, her life was symmetrical and colour-coded, and she somehow managed to keep all her balls up in the air all the time. Since Loulou had arrived, Sallie didn't feel the same way. She knew it was only a phase and tried to keep in mind that underneath the sleep deprivation, she was the same person, but she'd begun to feel a little bit as if she was constantly chasing her tail.

Maisy bustled past, balancing mugs of hot chocolate. 'Hiya. How are you? All ready for the carol service? Folks in here have been talking about it nonstop. Is everything organised and ready to go?'

'I hope so. I'll settle for no catastrophes,' Sallie joked.

'Lucian was in here yesterday. He said the world will be watching. Suntanned Pete said he's as proud as punch.'

Sallie forced a smile, though her stomach gave a horrible, revolting, nervous lurch. A snuffle and the tiniest squeak emerged from the pram and both women froze. Sallie reached down, adjusted the blanket, wiggled the pram handle and held her breath. Loulou gave a sigh, turned her head, and settled again. 'Nobody move. Nobody breathe,' Sallie whispered and chuckled.

'Nobody speak,' Nina laughed.

At that moment, a group of ladies from the gardening club tumbled in, snow in their hair, scarves trailing. They laughed and chatted as they queued at the counter, and the café seemed to glow with Christmas warmth. As Nina chatted to Maisy, Sallie looked around and thought about how much she loved the little Pretty Beach community. It gave her a sense of assurance that the carol service would indeed go well. What was happening in the café was the bit the cameras couldn't fake: the hum, the kindness, the chat, the small-town glow. It was why, in the early days of being in Pretty Beach, she had been reeled in.

Feeling her shoulders drop a fraction, Sallie pursed her lips together. Maybe Nina was right. Maybe Pretty Beach would work its magic as it usually did, meaning she had absolutely nothing to worry about. Licking cream from her spoon, she glanced at the pram and inhaled an enormous breath, hoping that everything would turn out well. *Please, just hold for one beautiful night.*

4

A few days or so later, Sallie replied to a message from Ben about Loulou's naptime and closed the door of her car just outside The Orangery. As she gathered her market basket and turned around, the sight of the old building absolutely took her breath away. It had caused the same reaction from her since the day she'd first set eyes on it. However, covered in a dusting of snow with little sparkly pops twinkling here and there, it was simply magnificent.

Its lovely vintage weathervane on the top caught her eye as it turned this way and that, and as she looked upwards, it went through Sallie's mind just how far she'd come since she'd bought the old building. At that stage in her life and not long after arriving in Pretty Beach, she'd been on both a tight budget and journey to new things. What she hadn't known then, when she'd gambled on The Orangery, was that it would turn out to be one of her better decisions in life. The lovely old place had meant that her events business had gone from strength to strength right from the word go. Nowadays, all her venues were booked out for most of the year and her spaces were always in demand. Sallie felt as if the beautiful glass building was not only part of her life, but one of her best friends. Not a bad thing, to be frank.

Sallie, no fool, had seen an opportunity with The Orangery, had swooped in and gone for her life. Now, she had a well-oiled team of people under her wing, a structured formula, and most of her events ran like clockwork. However, the carol service was a different kettle of fish for many reasons. Because of its status in the Pretty Beach annual calendar and because it was being filmed, the pressure was on and Sallie was feeling it. She just hoped that the stunning old glass building would play the game and do its thing. It had never really let her down before. Hopefully, it wouldn't decide now was a good time to change its tune.

The podcast and broadcast were not the only reasons our Sallie was feeling ragged. Juggling her business with the running of a house and the loving of a baby was proving a challenge. Before Loulou had arrived, she'd assumed she'd continue on doing the same old thing, but she'd underestimated just about everything. The culmination of all of the above meant that underneath what she showed on the surface, she was all out of sorts. Pushing through the gates, she smiled; she might be stretched thin and nervous about the event, but the old building sparkled. On either side of The Orangery's doors, two huge pots held tall Christmas trees covered from top to bottom in white, sparkly Christmas twinkles. Old-fashioned, black coach lights flanked the doors, and the apple trees to the right of the garden area drowned in warm-white cluster lights. If there was one thing Sallie did well, it was Christmas decorating, and the outside of The Orangery showcased her talent like a mother.

After hustling down the snow-covered path, Sallie opened the door to the main area, flicked on the switches by the front door, and, despite her worries about the event, she beamed and let out a sigh of relief as the aesthetics hit her right between the eyes. The old glass building looked *spectacular*. It had taken a lot of planning, much thought, gambles on budget, and a shedload of brainpower, mostly hers, to get it how it now appeared, but boy, did it drop Christmas in one fell swoop. Just about everything sparkled. Thousands of white lights crisscrossed the vaulted roof, and on every shelf, surface, windowsill, and high ledge, a mismatched jumble of lanterns was filled with tiny electric tealights ready to be lit.

Sallie walked around, pleased with her hard work and paused by the old woodburner in the corner. The woodburner was one of her favourite things; when roaring and doing its thing, she loved how it crackled, glowed and soothed and had been the talking point at many a function. Peering outside, she mentally ticked off items on her list, including a small backup generator, half-hidden behind a drape of ivy, which was tucked up and ready if needed. Suntanned Pete had wheeled it in the week before, and she'd wondered if he was being over the top, but as the snow pressed harder against the glass roof, she was grateful for well-made plans.

Together with the lanterns and the lights, thick garlands of pine filled the space here, there and everywhere. Sallie had gambled on the purchase of offcuts from a local Christmas tree farm and had turned them into garlands that now swathed the entire room. Ben had rigged up a system to suspend them from the ceiling and they surrounded the perimeter of The Orangery in a swirl of gorgeous festive green. Giving her a whole lot of bang for her buck, Sallie had done well on the offcuts bet. The smell, let alone the appearance, was nothing short of wondrous. At least she'd got one thing right.

Slowly walking around the edge of the room, she started to check things as she made her way to the back of the building. Tugging a sprig of greenery here, straightening a lantern there, she scanned every ledge and corner looking for issues. She'd planned, strategised, and worked her behind off so that the festive decorating looked and felt effortless. Right from the word go, she had wanted The Orangery to feel as if its festive dressing had fallen into place with a sprinkle of fairy dust, like walking through a Christmas wonderland without a care in the world. For certain, she'd achieved it. Surrounding her, a decadence of white lights, looping green garlands, beautiful silk ribbons and a walloping great tree wowed. Sallie had absolutely pulled it off beyond measure; there was no doubt about that.

It had, however, come at a cost. She was the walking, talking, very tired, aching in areas she didn't know she had, reality of the feat that was now in front of her eyes. There'd been long nights, early mornings, and a lot more work than she'd anticipated. Hours and hours had gone into wiring garlands, balancing lanterns, erecting the tree with guy ropes and fixing lights. She'd planned every votive holder, tealight, and bunch of mistletoe, and now her hard work looked back at her. Pausing beneath the main part of the vaulted ceiling, she tilted her head back, looked up, and inhaled the pine scent from the garlands. Talk about smelling like Christmas. The garlands dropped the Christmas fir scent better than any candle could ever even hope to achieve. A crisscross of white lights glittered, reflected in the glass panes, and thousands of tiny stars twinkled against the winter afternoon. For sure, Sallie was exhausted by it all, but for a moment, she just smiled, wallowed, and nodded her head in recognition of a job well done. It looked more than good. The Orangery, dressed in its Christmas finery, was, in fact, *spellbinding.*

'Sallie! There you are!' Lucian, owner of the podcast, Where the Heck is Pretty Beach? knew how to make an entrance. Sweeping in with a scarf draped extravagantly around his neck, a beanie hat pulled low, and a little glint of earrings, Lucian hustled in from the cold. With a camera bag over one shoulder and two tripods under his arm, he shook his head. 'Brr. It's *freezing* out there. It looks like more snow is on the way. Goodness, could we have asked for better timing for a sprinkling of the white stuff? Though we need it to stop now. Am I right, darling?'

Sallie beamed. Lucian always brightened her day. Funny, kind, and all around gorgeous, he was a lovely addition to Sallie's life. 'You re always right. Yes, let's hope our luck lasts. What we have now is perfect. We don't want a blizzard.'

Spinning slowly in a circle, Lucian blinked and smiled. 'My goodness, this building is dazzling, darling. Razzle dazzle. Now everything is in place, it rocks.'

'You think?'

'For sure. You've outdone yourself, darling. It's like stepping inside a *living* Christmas card. You said it would look amazing and you weren't wrong. The garlands are outstanding! I did wonder what your vision was with them, but yes, you nailed it. I knew you would. Oh, the smell! It's absolutely amazing in here. Even better than it was the other day.'

Sallie laughed, though her nerves flickered. 'Let's just hope it holds together once everyone's in here. What do you think? Do you think it will work on camera?'

Lucian placed the tripods carefully against the wall, whipped his beanie off and ran his hand through his hair. Pointing upwards with both hands, he wiggled his head. 'Honey, it won't just work. It will sing! This ceiling or roof or whatever that is alone is going to break the internet. People are going to be sobbing into their eggnog from here to New York. The garlands are genius! And the light bounces from those lanterns like nothing else. Gosh, the tree is *ginormous*, darling. Honestly, the BBC could take notes on this. Although I have to say and I am not blowing my own trumpet, well maybe just a little bit, that my reach is far, far more than the BBC these days. And after that debacle with them recently, well, let's not go there.'

Sallie let out a small sigh of relief that Lucian was clearly impressed. 'You're sure? You know I can't see it through a lens the way you do. I've done so much of this now that, to be quite frank, I am sick of the sight of pine and fir. If I find another needle in my sock, I'll scream.'

Lucian chuckled and clapped his hands. 'I'm hearing you, but we're on the home straight already.'

Sallie smiled. 'I'm going to need a lot of mulled wine once we're through this. I'll be having it with my tea in the morning.'

'You and I both, darling. In fact, I need a drop of brandy in my coffee today, I do believe.' Lucian bustled around, pulling cables from his bag and flicking switches on a camera. 'Trust me. I've been doing tests all week.' He gestured theatrically around the room. 'I've got three extra angles I've been testing. I think it'll be good if we set up here, here, and there, and I've brought in a roving one for the choir. We've scoped out every corner. Don't panic, we'll keep it discreet. No one will even know we're here.'

'I trust you, millions wouldn't,' Sallie joked.

'Sal, this could go viral, I don't mean Lucian-viral, I mean viral-viral. The Orangery is going to fly.'

'Cripes, you're making me more nervous. How in the world do you sleep at night with the job you do?'

'I'm a *machine*. Anyway, I want the world to see Pretty Beach in all its finery, that's how I got myself into this in the first place.'

'Ha.'

'How's the lovely Loulou today? Will she be gracing us with her presence?'

Sallie shook her head. 'Nope, she will not.'

'Aww, I love her. She's so pretty and funny.'

Sallie followed Lucian as he moved, energy pouring off him. Only Lucian could make livestream logistics look theatrical and interesting. 'She is, but she's also in charge when she's here...'

'Yes, good point. Okay, so we're pretty much ready to go and broadcast ourselves to millions live.'

'Ahh, I'm trying to tell myself this is just our little carol service, you know? When I think about how many people might watch this, I'm like a bag of nerves. There are so many things that could go wrong.'

Lucian whirled, eyes bright. 'Oh no, darling, don't say that! This is not just any old *little* thing. This is a Christmas shindig for my podcast, which is now not just a podcast as it once was, but a media entity in its own right. This carol service will be amazing and the whole world is going to know it.'

Sallie shuddered and closed her eyes. 'Ahh, I've been fooling myself that it'll just be a few hundred people watching.'

Lucian raised his eyebrows as he unspooled a length of cable with a flourish. 'I would *not* be doing this if I were not guaranteed millions of views. It wouldn't be worth my time, darling. These days, I don't get out of bed for, well, not unless it will generate a lot of money.'

Sallie trailed after him and gulped. *Too late to back out now.*

Lucian continued, clearly oblivious to Sallie's nerves. 'It even *smells* divine in here. Pine, fir, all the Christmas smells. Our darling organiser has outdone herself every which way. This place is ready for *millions* of pairs of eyeballs, darling. Bring it on.'

Sallie gave him a look. 'Just what I need to hear, not.'

Lucian grinned, unbothered. 'My lovely mummy always told me that nerves are good, darling. They sharpen you, is what she always liked to tell me. Besides, no one will notice you trembling when they're all crying into their scarves at "Silent Night" and the beauty of that enormous Christmas tree.'

Sallie thought about how the Christmas tree had its own guy ropes and that she wasn't totally convinced that it would stay upright. As she crouched to straighten a lantern, she cringed. 'I just hope everything stays where it should and all the camera stuff works.'

Lucian clicked his tongue. 'Please, my audio assistant has tested every cable three times. We've got backup batteries, backup mics and internet, backup everything short of a second choir. Suntanned Pete supplied that generator. For someone who is an expert in organisation, you worry too much.'

'I've done a lot of events. Things go wrong.'

'So have I. Darling, I have flair to rely on if anything goes pear-shaped.' Lucian spread his arms, as if to prove his point.

'You are nothing if not confident. Yikes, mind the tree.'

Lucian gave a bow. 'It's why I'm successful. Sorry, sorry. I'll stay an inch away from the foliage at all times.'

Sallie tugged at a swathe of greenery that had gone a bit lopsided as Lucian crouched to plug in a camera. 'If this lot comes down on everyone, I am going to need more than liability insurance.'

Lucian looked up at a star on top of the tree. 'That up there deserves its own Instagram account. You really *have* done well. This, darling, is Pretty Beach history, right here, right now. You'll thank me when we're trending.'

Sallie shook her head, but inside, there was a little spark of pride. It had to be said that The Orangery *did* look spectacular. Even *she* had to admit it.

'The world's going to fall in love with us. Look at this place. It's like Narnia, but with better lighting.'

'Let's just hope it all goes smoothly.'

Lucian rolled his eyes. 'Sweetheart, it's going to go beautifully because you've made it so lovely and you've backed that talent up with planning. That's how the best events go off with a bang.' Lucian stepped back and gave a satisfied sigh, brushing imaginary dust off his trousers. 'You, my dear, are way too modest. It's the English in you.' He gestured around The Orangery. 'This is a triumph, and when the choir starts, the snow's falling outside, and my livestream hits a gazillion views, you'll remember this moment and think, Lucian was right, as usual.'

Sallie gulped. 'I hope so.'

Lucian straightened. 'It's nearly showtime, darling. Pretty Beach is going to sparkle. Let's rock and roll.'

Sallie exhaled and glanced around the room. Fairy lights flickered, the scent of pine hung in the air, and the tree glittered. She, however, did not feel that confident. At all. Rather, she had a horrible feeling that something was going to go very, very wrong.

5

It was five-thirty in the morning and the day of the carol service. Sallie woke to the sound of what she assumed were pellets of sleet hitting the bedroom window. At any other time, she would have been more than pleased by this occurrence. This time, not so much. A big deal was going on outside. It didn't sound like the soft, picturesque dusting of snow that had been falling for the previous few days, but rather, proper, relentless, life-changing snow. The kind of snow that wasn't puffed into cosy romcom movies where the leads walked along with hot chocolates in their hands and beanies on their heads. Nope, it was more the sort of snow that sounded as if it meant trouble. Of course, it had felt the need to come down hard when Sallie had prayed for the soft, easy, fluffy flurries of sparkly snowflakes made by hand in Hollywood. At least it had made an appearance, she supposed.

Rolling over, she squinted at the grey light filtering through the curtains and quietly groaned as what was going on outside the window dropped fully into her brain.

Ben stirred beside her. 'What's wrong?'

'Listen. This is *not* good.'

Ben propped himself up on one elbow and tilted his head. 'I can't hear her.'

'Not Loulou. She won't be awake for ages. Listen to what is going on out there. It will be chaos on the roads.'

'What?'

'Outside.' Sallie raised her chin in the direction of the window.

Right at that second, the wind rattled the glass, and it sounded as if the snow was coming down in thick, heavy sheets that knocked on the window panes. 'Ah. Oh dear. I see what you mean.'

'Yep. You *know* that I *know* snow and this is not great for the event.' Pushing back the duvet, Sallie pulled on her thick winter dressing gown and padded to the window. Shaking her head, she sighed as she took in the scene. Outside, Strawberry Hill was submerged under several inches of white. For sure, it was strikingly beautiful, but it was also burying everything it could. The lane had disappeared and trees bowed under the weight of a heavy fall. It looked so very pretty, of course it did, and on any other given pre-Christmas stretch, Sallie would have welcomed it, loved it, adored it, positively inhaled it. However, today, the absolute beauty of the white stuff falling from the sky in droves was the last thing she needed. She had an event to run and didn't need any complications whatsoever.

Ben appeared behind her and rested his hand on her shoulder. 'How bad is it? Oh dear, right, yeah, that's not great. It's really come down and settled since we went to bed.'

'Bad enough to affect travel and logistics. Oh well, we can deal with it. We've planned for it.' Sallie checked the weather app on her phone. The forecast had changed overnight. What had been a light dusting was now a full-blown blizzard, with warnings plastered across her phone screen in red. Tapping along the top of her screen, she shook her head. Heavy snowfall was expected throughout the day and travel disruptions were predicted, expected and likely. Sallie's stomach dropped. 'When I prayed for snow, I wanted a sweet and cosy dusting of sparkly glitter bombs all over the place. This is not what I ordered. The deliveries and everything won't go well in this.'

Ben kissed the top of her head. 'They'll get through.'

'Will they?'

'Pretty Beach doesn't shut down for a bit of snow. I *do* know that.'

'Ben, this isn't a *bit* of snow. This is a *lot* of snow. This is the kind of snow that stops lorries and closes roads and ruins things. If it carries on at this rate, we'll need to cancel the carol service. I've invested so much money into this. It's not even worth thinking about how much.'

Ben squeezed Sallie's shoulders. 'Let's not panic yet.' He checked his watch. 'Crikey, it's still *very* early.'

Sallie nodded. 'I wanted to get a head start on everything.'

Ben put his fingers to his lips. 'You did that alright. We don't want to wake the princess, otherwise she'll be crotchety as hell later, and we'll both have to deal with the fallout.'

'I know. I was going to creep down and leave you both asleep. I put my clothes in the downstairs bathroom last night just in case.'

'Come on, I'll make tea.'

Sallie nodded, however, inside, she was already running through her lists. She had a delayed champagne order arriving, a food delivery from Holly's bakery, and the Pretty Beach choir was meant to be gathering for a final rehearsal run-through. The carol service itself was all set up and ready to go from her end, but the weather situation made logistics precarious. She had to pull the evening off without a hitch, but it looked as if the weather was going to do its level best to sabotage her. Whispering to Ben, she pointed to the bed. 'Honestly, you go back to sleep. It's going to be a long day. I'll go down and make myself some tea in peace and sit and go through my lists. There's no point in us both getting up, especially if you're going to be cooped up all day here with Loulou.'

Ben looked at the bed and raised his eyebrows. 'Sure?'

'Yes, I'm happy to sit and go through everything quietly and I'll get ready downstairs. It might be easier if I walk in. I got my wellies ready last night just in case.'

Ben tried to hide his glee at going back to bed. 'If you're sure. I don't mind coming down to make you tea.'

'Yeah, no.' Sallie joked. 'Put it in the sleep bank and I'll cash it in later.'

Downstairs, as she walked into the kitchen, Sallie smiled at how festive it looked. If a room was ever going to be able to make her happy, the kitchen at Christmas was it. The heating hummed, the Aga glowed, a Christmas tree sparkled from the corner and outside, the snow kept falling. As she took a recycled jam jar filled with overnight oats out of the fridge, she watched as the snow hit the window and the back lawn. Dumping the contents of the jar into a saucepan, she slid it onto the Aga and checked her phone. According to the Pretty Beach Facebook page, the roads were still open, but for how long? She'd been doing events long enough to know that weather was normally something that turned everything upside down. Chaos was brewing. Sallie could feel it in her bones.

Sitting with her cup of tea and warm oats, she crossed her fingers that the snowfall would ease. But as she stood up, walked over to the back door and leant on the architrave, thick, heavy, very pretty flurries of snowflakes fell harder and harder. It did not bode well.

6

On hearing nothing from Loulou, Sallie had showered in the downstairs bathroom to give Ben as long a lie-in as possible and was making her way down the hill in the direction of the laneway running through the centre of Pretty Beach. Rugged up in a huge scarf, velvet jeans tucked into Hunter wellies, a slouchy beanie and a pea coat, she was dressed both for the weather and a day at work. Thankfully, the roads had been salted, so at least most of Pretty Beach was still on the move. Keeping to a cleared pavement, she stopped by a stone wall capped with a good few inches of snow settled on the top and sent a message to Ben.

Sallie: *I listened at the bottom of the stairs, but you still weren't up, so I left you. I'm heading to The Orangery on foot (wellies on). I didn't want to chance driving. It looks like the roads have been salted and gritted, so it's not too bad. I need to check the heating and make sure everything's ready.*

Ben: *She's just woken up. Call me if you need anything. x*

Sallie pulled her coat tighter, fastened the funnel-neck top and wrapped her scarf more snugly around her neck. The walk down the hill took twice as long as usual as she carefully watched every step. Blowing out little puffs of smoke into the air in front of her, Pretty Beach, wrapped in a shroud of sparkly white, took her breath away. Despite a few people here and there and cars inching past, a muffled quietness hung over the rooftops as the snow hushed everything in its wake. The pavements were slippery, the wind cut through her layers, and by the time Sallie had reached The Orangery's gates, her fingers and the end of her nose were numb.

Pushing through, she unlocked the main door, and as she stepped inside, warmth hit her immediately. At least the heating was working; there was that. The Orangery glowed in the low morning light, the garlands and fairy lights exactly as she'd left them the day before, lanterns placed just so, the Christmas tree towering. As she stamped her feet on the doormat and looked around, she had to admit one thing; it looked nothing short of perfect. She'd been aiming for perfection. Seemed she'd nigh-on achieved it.

Flicking on the switches and watching the place light up, a pang of dread landed in Sallie's stomach as she looked up at a heavy blanket of white on the glass roof. The amount of snow that had fallen and still continued to pile on spelt trouble as far as she was concerned. She had a funny feeling that the event was not going to happen or that something was going to go *horribly* wrong. That all her effort, months of planning, and weeks of decorating, would end up marooned under a heavy blanket of white.

Her phone buzzed. A text from the champagne supplier, which told her that the delivery was having trouble leaving its starting point. Sallie stared at the screen, tutted and shook her head. A lack of fancy French bubbles wasn't a deal-breaker at the end of the day. The whole success of the evening was less about champagne and more about the aesthetics of the night and how much the community enjoyed it. Her backup plan without bubbles was to double up on the mulled wine and leave it at that. So much for fancy bubbles. Mulled wine would most definitely be better on her budget anyway.

Walking to the Christmas tree, she checked the lights and thought about everything that had been planned. The impact of the event on the live feed hinged on thousands of flickering candles, the over-the-top nature of the garlands and the in-your-face presence of the Christmas tree. Apart from that, at the end of the day, all that was really needed was the choir. She just didn't want them to get stuck somewhere on the other side of Pretty Beach in a snowdrift and not turn up. It was fairly tricky to have a carol service without a choir.

She rang Holly from the bakery about the cinnamon bun delivery scheduled for later that day. 'Hey, Holly. Morning. How is it with you?'

Holly sounded frazzled. 'We're still open, but it's coming down thick and fast here. I've had two girls call in that they can't get through from the hills because the gritters didn't make it up there in the night. We should be okay, though, once the roads are treated. What a turn up for the books.'

Sallie closed her eyes briefly. When Holly sounded frazzled, you needed to worry. 'Oh dear. Do you need any help?'

'What, while you're trying to organise a carol service?'

'Ha.'

'No, we're fine. You know me, I have things running like clockwork, two staff down or not. I've had to get Mum off her trading app this morning and into the office. She's not a happy bunny about that, but what can you do?'

'Please tell me your delivery is still happening.'

Holly's voice was bright and unbothered. 'Of course! Worst comes to the worst, we'll use the four-wheel drive, or we'll push the stuff around in a trolley. We'll be there like we said. You know you can count on us.'

Sallie sighed in relief. 'Great, thanks. I can't have this event without Locals Only cinnamon buns. I'll never live it down.'

'You're not wrong. Any problems your end?'

'The champagne isn't coming today by the looks of it.'

'Really? I thought you would have had that sorted out ages ago.'

'It *was* sorted out months ago by me, but I used a new supplier. This is the second time they've messed up. Never again.'

'Is it delayed because of the snow?'

'That's their excuse this time. Supposedly, they can't get through. The road is closed at their end.'

There was a pause. 'Right. Okay. Don't panic. We'll sort something. Leave it with me. I'll ask around. Someone in this town will have a stash of bubbles. It's Pretty Beach.'

Sallie chuckled. 'Thanks, Hol, but to be honest, I'm going to Plan B, which is mulled wine. It will be fine.'

'Yeah, in this weather, that sounds better anyway. It's going to be okay.'

'I'm not holding my breath.'

'No going back now. I bet Lucian is having kittens! Rightio, see you later.'

Sallie hung up, leant against the doorframe and peered out at the snow. Everything was fine on the surface, and thankfully, she'd thought about all the things that could go wrong. Snow was still falling, the champagne hadn't arrived, and she had a sinking feeling it was only the beginning of what was going to be a very busy day.

~

By ten o'clock, Holly had worked a miracle. She'd rallied half the town, and within the hour, a steady stream of locals had arrived at The Orangery with bottles of bubbly. Mismatched, certainly, but it was enough to see Sallie through. In fact, by the end of it, she was drowning in champagne. As she was fussing with a set of lights by the tree, Juliette, local midwife, arrived. Juliette, self-confessed Christmas addict, owned an online Christmas shop and had partnered with Sallie to decorate The Orangery for the festive season. With a gigantic basket over her arm, and bundled up in a huge pale pink coat, pink bobble hat and pink wellies, Juliette was full of the joys of the season as she beamed. 'Morning, Sal. Well, it's certainly snowing, there's no question about that.'

'Morning. I did pray for snow, just not this much.' Sallie rolled her eyes. 'It doesn't appear to be letting up.'

Putting her basket on a table near the door, Juliette pulled off her gloves. 'I've brought more cinnamon sticks, star anise, and a bag of cloves so we can make more mulled wine after your text.'

'Holly rallied the troops, and I've had bottles of bubbles arriving from all over the place. We'll still do more mulled wine, though, because of the weather.'

Juliette shook her head. 'She's a one! Only *she* could rustle up champagne from nowhere.'

'I know. I thought the same thing.'

'We'll still do the mulled wine. We need this place to smell like Christmas from three streets away and it'll do that.'

Sallie lifted the cloth on Juliette's basket and smiled. 'You angel. We will win everyone over with the scent of all that, even if they have to crunch through a blizzard to get here.'

'Who would have thought it would come down as much as it has? It wasn't forecast to be this heavy.' Juliette frowned as she looked out the window.

'I know. We just need to pray that the road doesn't shut. Half the choir lives over the other side.'

Juliette grimaced 'Oh my God! We'll have to sing! That will not be good for anyone in any shape or form.'

'God help us all. I'm like a drowned rat when I sing. Not that anyone would refer to it as "singing".'

'Ha. It doesn't bear thinking about. Right, where do you want me?'

'Filling the rest of the jam jars with the remaining tealights. I ordered extra because I need this place to literally twinkle. I did a run through a couple of days ago and there just weren't enough.'

Juliette nodded. 'Right. Let's do this. Last push. My mission is to fully glitter up Pretty Beach.'

7

A couple of hours later, Sallie looked around The Orangery as she pulled a box out from under a table and handed it to Juliette. The huge tree stood glorious, overpowering and overdone, exactly as she'd intended, and the blanket of white outside added to the festive feel. A sweep of tartan used as a tree skirt caught the light and hundreds of thousands of tiny gleams of sparkle glinted all around The Orangery. The old building grumbled as a gust of wind pressed snow against the glass and both Sallie and Juliette looked up at the roof as it creaked.

Juliette spoke first. 'Yikes, there's a lot of snow up there. Do you think we should shift some of it from the outside? I don't like the look of all that weight on the panes.'

'I thought the same earlier. I messaged Suntanned Pete, and apparently, he has a roof rake, not that I know what one of those is. He said he'll pop over. I'm quietly terrified about cracked glass and sleet inside during what is supposed to be a carol service full of joy and festivity.'

'Suntanned Pete to the rescue as usual. He certainly puts in his pound of flesh for this town.'

'One can hope.' Sallie's phone buzzed; she looked down and raised her eyebrows. 'Speak of the devil. This is him now.'

Pete: *Roads are passable in town. Outliers stuck in the hills. Be with you shortly.*

'He must have heard us. He's on his way. Okay, you carry on with that. I'm going to go out the back and check how the pipes are out there. I don't really know what to look for, but I can try.'

Walking around the perimeter of the building, Sallie checked the radiators, then the door seals in the back room, then walked through to the kitchen and put the kettle on. Checking a list on her iPad, she tallied it up with two pages of notes on a clipboard, added "salt steps and front entrance," and underlined it. Just after she'd made a pot of tea and was helping Juliette with the lanterns, the front door opened a crack, and a blast of cold air whipped in, carrying snowflakes with it. Suntanned Pete in wraparound metallic sunglasses, a bobble hat, oversized tartan flannel shirt and raw cheeks from the wind poked his head around the door. 'Morning. Yeah, that roof looks heavy. I've got my ladders with me and the roof rake is in the back of the van.'

Sallie smiled. 'Morning. I just put some tea in the pot, Pete. Do you want one?'

Pete shook his head and jerked his thumb at the snow. 'I'll do the roof first, I think, and have tea after. I'd better get up there pronto. It's coming down thick and fast.' With that, Pete turned on his heel and disappeared into the flurries of snow tumbling from a full grey-white sky.

A few minutes later, Juliette and Sallie watched Pete put up some ladders and then saw his boots pass the high panes. Each time the brush scraped, Sallie held her breath. Lowering her voice, she looked up. 'What were we thinking, letting him go up there alone? We'll be lucky if he doesn't fall through. It must be so slippery up there. Did he even do any risk assessment? He doesn't have any safety gear or anything! I will never forgive myself if anything happens to him.'

Juliette shuddered and blinked rapidly. 'Hopefully, he knows what he's doing. The last thing we need is Pete with broken bones. He looks very precarious up there.'

'My brain can't deal with even thinking about it.'

Juliette squinted upwards. 'Well, if nothing else, that is the Pretty Beach way working its magic right there in front of our eyes.'

Sallie chuckled. 'True. He's so kind to everyone.'

Juliette nodded. 'Pretty Beach runs on favours in and favours out. That's why I like it here. Hopefully, I won't be initiating my medical skills when he falls straight through the roof. You're right, there is no way we should have let him go up without any help.'

'Fingers crossed he's okay. I'm well versed in the Pretty Beach way nowadays.' Sallie chuckled and sipped her tea.

'Okay, I'll get on with putting the bits and bobs out for the mulled wine and let's just hope we don't see his boots through the glass.'

Half an hour later, Suntanned Pete came in with a face full of snow and a huge grin. 'Right, that wasn't too tricky. It just slid off and landed out the back there. The roof looks a lot safer now. I cleared the worst. The back slope still has a drift over there where the hedge meets it, but it won't press the glass.'

'You are a star,' Sallie sighed. 'Thank you *so* much.'

Juliette agreed. 'You are. Did you do that whole job in sunnies?'

Pete nodded and slid his sunglasses up so they perched on his hat. 'I did. They double as safety wear.'

'Ha.' Juliette giggled. 'You crack me up, Pete.'

'We realised you shouldn't have gone up there like that without anyone else and no ropes or anything.'

Pete wrinkled his nose and waved his hand in dismissal. 'Don't be silly. I've done worse than that in my time.'

'On top of a glass roof?'

'To be fair, it was a bit dicey.'

Sallie raised her eyebrows in question. 'Tea?'

'Thought you'd never ask.'

All three of them made their way through The Orangery to the kitchen and Sallie made three mugs of tea. Taking one, Pete stood near a radiator. 'The laneway is fine and passable and most of the roads are gritted. Up past your way and into the hills, it gets sketchy. I met the vicar on the way, and she said the hills will most likely be cut off if it continues like this. I agree. That's usually how it goes.'

Sallie nodded. 'In terms of who gets here from the choir, we'll just have to work with what we've got.'

'What's left to do?' Pete asked.

'Not much. I need to put the overflow chairs out, salt the path and warm the mulled wine later. Yeah, everything else is sorted. If only I could stop the snow from falling quite as hard as it is.'

Pete chuckled. 'Well, it certainly feels like Christmas. The snow, the candles, the vibe in here. It's going to be spectacular if you ask me.'

Sallie smiled. 'Hope so.'

'Hope? Sallie, it is a certainty. Trust me.'

8

It wasn't long until the choir's warm-up. Sallie checked her watch and felt as if her pulse was keeping time with the second hand. Outside The Orangery and around Pretty Beach, snow continued to fall. All-consuming, it most definitely meant business as big, weighty clusters tumbled from the sky. The kind of snowfall that almost swallowed sound and settled as soon as it landed. Standing at the Orangery door with her phone in her hand and a knot in her stomach, she felt as if her nerves were frayed at the end. The gravel path had blurred under a white quilt, the hedges were weighed down with white, and the glass roof wore a lacework of not only a new layer of snow but now frost had joined it too. Beautiful, yes, good for logistics, not in the slightest.

Her weather app refreshed, and Sallie gulped as she saw a red band march over Pretty Beach, appearing to swallow it whole. Checking the time, she went through the run sheet in her head and crossed her fingers that things would go well. Not that long until the choir's warm-up, then the doors would open, and shortly after that, the first carol would commence. She sent up a small prayer to every saint who had ever cared about events that it would go well. A little birdie whispered that something was going to go wrong.

The snow was thick and unrelenting, feathering everywhere Sallie looked. Glancing at the huge old clock above the main doors, she decided there was nothing she could do about the weather other than stop stressing about it. It wouldn't be long until she'd need to get changed, then guests would arrive, the livestream would be set to roll, and Lucian's precious sponsors would be dialling in from London and goodness-knows-where. Somewhere between now and then, she still had to re-salt the path, set up the cinnamon buns after they'd been delivered from the bakery, check the mulled-wine urns, sort out Loulou when she arrived with Ben, and remember to breathe.

Ben had said all along that it didn't have to be perfect, but Sallie couldn't help herself from wanting just that. Ever since having Loulou, she'd felt she owed someone or something some sort of proof that she could still deliver and get everything right. Gulping in anticipation, she told herself it was just the cold, the rush of snow and the stress that was making her feel nervous, but really it was because she wanted to pull off an amazing event.

A message landed from Holly.

Holly: *The road from the bakery to you looks dicey. A van is stuck on Church Lane. I've split the order. Mum is on foot with the cinnamon buns in a trolley and one of my girls is behind her with the sausage rolls. Don't panic.*

Sallie closed her eyes for half a second, replied to Holly and continued to stand by the door, fretting. Lucian came from behind the centre aisle with a cable in one hand and a tape measure in the other. 'We have a situation, one of my assistants is stuck on the dual-carriageway miles away. She has the spare gimbal and batteries and she is much better at filming the cut-offs than I am. Not a problem, I can film, but yeah, not great.'

'We talked about all these possibilities. Hopefully, she'll still get here, though, looking at that blizzard out there, it might not happen. Thank goodness we had meetings about things not going to plan.' Sallie tutted. 'You couldn't make this up if you tried.'

'Yep, just call us professionals. What's happened about the buns?'

'I just heard from Holly. They are now arriving on foot because a van is blocking a road.'

Lucian pressed his lips together. 'I shall pretend to cry on stream. People adore grit and adversity. They donate more when they see grit.'

Sallie giggled. 'You crack me up.'

Lucian gave a small bow. 'Right, well, I will put Plan X into place and we'll go from there.' At a noise outside, he looked in the direction of the gates. 'Looks like that's the cinnamon buns now.'

Xian, in a huge Christmas jumper with a lit-up reindeer nose, bright purple wellies and a yellow sou'wester fisherman's hat, shuffled in pushing a trolley in front of her. 'All clear! I come bearing joy, cinnamon, and myrrh.'

Sallie could have kissed her. 'You are a queen. Nice hat.'

Xian took a small silver hip flask out of her pocket, popped it to her lips, took a quick nip and gestured to the gates. 'The sausage rolls will be here soon.'

'Thank you so much. You should have called; one of us would have come and collected them.'

'No, no, all good. I needed to get out. It's utter madness in the bakery.'

Juliette swept past with a basket of white ribbons looped over her arm. She'd already dressed the aisle lanterns and was now partaking in some last-minute fussing at the tree with a handful of white and gold silk bows. Juliette was nothing if not a perfectionist; handy because she was in good company. Each knot on the bows sat perfectly, every lantern was angled just so, and the fir garlands had been fiddled with until they were exquisite.

Lucian called out a countdown to no one in particular and bent to a camera on a low tripod where a red tally light winked. He paced back three steps, lifted his hands as if conducting, then glanced at his screen. 'Yes, the angles are delicious,' he announced to the rafters. 'We may not have my chief assistant, but until my prodigal returns, we make do. Hiya Xian. Thanks for trudging through with those.'

Sallie took the trolley from Xian and nudged it through the side corridor to the kitchen. Inside white cardboard cake boxes under a linen cloth, lines of tiny Christmas cinnamon buns doused in gold glitter sat in perfectly neat, exceedingly delicious-looking rows. The smell that escaped as she lifted the lid nearly knocked Sallie over. Have cinnamon buns, event will go well.

'Voilà,' Xian cackled. 'Locals Only Christmas cinnamon buns. Our mini versions are only made for very special occasions, as you well know. They've been dusted with edible gold glitter. You're welcome.'

Sallie laughed and leaned over the boxes. Each bun sat perfectly swirled, glossy with icing, and little gold flecks caught the light. 'Oh my goodness, look at them! They're *utterly* perfect.'

Xian pulled the small silver hip flask out of her pocket again, held it over her lips and let its contents glug into her mouth. 'They'll go down well afterwards. They always do.'

Sallie smiled and nodded her head. 'These are exactly what we need. Glittery morale to keep us all going. Give us blizzards, we'll give you sparkly cinnamon buns.'

Xian peered into one of the boxes. 'They *do* look good, actually. Between us, we'll be trending on the socials. Pretty Beach is going to show the world how it's done.'

Sallie gulped and hoped Xian was correct. 'Amen to that.'

9

Sallie was, without a doubt, dressed for the occasion. A lot of thought had been put into her outfit, as had the rest of the event. Sallie herself, whether out for a walk with Loulou or having a meeting at work, always *wanted* to look the part. Someone in her early life had continually rammed down her throat the importance of being well turned out, no matter one's place in the world. That same person had informed Sallie that, despite background, economic or employment status, being proud of how one presented set one well. It had been one of the few pieces of advice, and there hadn't been many, that had been solid in Sallie's world, and she'd always followed it to the letter. When she'd been on the bones of her you-know-what, she'd still made sure she was as well presented as possible. The advice had helped her in more ways than one. Tonight was no different. In fact, like the setting, the tree and the garlands, she razzle-dazzled. At least, on the outside anyway.

In terms of how she presented herself, nowadays, Sallie hadn't changed from the person who had first walked into Pretty Beach. It was just that the quality had gone up, her budget worries had all but disappeared, and many of the old demons that had been prevalent in her brain had been slayed. Truth be told, Sallie Broadchurch now played in a whole different ball game altogether. Her husband was worth a few bob, she lived in a very nice house in a very nice part of the world, and she didn't have to constantly rub two pennies together to try and make three. The brain power of having let that go was something else, a positive she couldn't put a price on and showed in how she was dressed for the event. Smoothing down her fitted velvet high-neck top and wide-leg trousers, she attempted to calm her racing heart and the fact that her hands were shaking. Twisting a diamond tennis bracelet Ben had given her when she'd had Loulou, she said a prayer that her outfit hid how nervous she was.

As she stood and looked around, she realised one thing was certain that no one could argue with: The Orangery couldn't really have looked better. The Christmas tree appeared as if it had been ordered by the man in red himself, the fir garlands filled the room with their gorgeous scent, and the tealights in their hundreds worked a treat. Even the chairs, with their white covers and gold baubles hanging on the back, were part of the aesthetics. Sallie, together with Juliette, had worked hard, and The Orangery was showing off about it.

Checking her watch, she did a final sweep of the room, gave a thumbs-up to Lucian and his crew minus his best assistant and raised her eyebrows at Juliette. Ben smiled from the door at the back and indicated that Loulou was dropping off to sleep. It seemed at least on the surface that all was well. Crossing her fingers in the pocket of her trousers that the snow would ease off, she walked through The Orangery, doing a few last things, poked her head around the door where Loulou's pram was and sent up a silent prayer that she would stay asleep. So far, so good. All was well.

Ten or so minutes later, the first guests started to arrive, with Holly from the bakery, full of herself, making a grand entrance. Dressed from head to toe in sparkle, with her mum Xian in tow, Holly could barely contain her excitement. Watching as Holly kissed Lucian, then Juliette, and hustled in, aiming for her reserved seat in the front row, Sallie smiled.

'Sallie! Oh me, oh my, you have outdone yourself. Juliette said it came up trumps, but this is something else. Well done, you. Wow! Mum mentioned it was amazing when she came over earlier. It looks spectacular in here. All ready?'

'As ready as we'll ever be.' Sallie laughed and pretended she was confident, sure of herself, in control. Inside, she was a bag of nerves, and her heart felt as if it were somewhere up near her throat. She swept her hand up and down Hollie's glittering outfit. 'You look like you've just stepped out of a Christmas bauble yourself. Holls, you are positively vibrating with sparkles.'

'Naturally, it's Christmas! I do it all year long; this is just the extra glammed-up festive version.' Holly twirled so her sparkly skirt caught the light. 'If you can't go all out at Christmas, when can you? I love this time of year! Give me all the glitter all the time.'

Sallie nodded as she giggled. 'You own it.'

'I do.' Holly raised her chin in the direction of the tree. 'The tree! My goodness, it's enormous! Did you actually grow it in here, ha ha? I would like to know the ins and outs of how you got that inside.' Holly cackled and joked. 'Nah, actually, I'd rather not know. It must have been a task and a half.'

Sallie glanced over at the tree. Holly wasn't wrong; it was ginormous and dominated the far end of The Orangery, just as she'd envisioned. Its tip brushed the glass ceiling, every branch dripped with lights and ribbons and Juliette's vintage glass ornaments shimmered in a jumble of gold and white. 'It does look a bit like it's about to burst through the roof, doesn't it?

Ben and Pete nearly lost fingers getting it in here. I'm really pleased with it.' Sallie omitted to add that she was concerned that it might fall down.

'Worth it.' Xian gazed up at it with her hands clasped together. 'It's like something out of one of those Christmas shows. The whole room is *absolutely* dazzling. I mean, The Orangery is already glorious, but this is amazing. You've outdone yourself this year, Sal. Every year I think you can't top it, and then you go and do this.' Xian shook her head. 'What can I say? The garlands alone…'

'Don't jinx me.' Sallie felt nerves flicker up and down her body. It was true that she'd pulled off some fabulous events since she'd been in Pretty Beach, but this one had been her most ambitious in terms of the decor. She'd had visions of the tree toppling onto the choir mid-carol and all sorts. 'We've still got to get through the whole evening without a light blowing the whole lot or someone tripping over Lucian's cables. Lots and lots of people are lined up to watch this on various platforms.'

'It'll be fine.'

'Loads of people have paid in Lucian's Members Only area to get a bird's eye view! Why do I do this to myself? Why?'

'Pfft.' Holly waved a glittery hand. 'If something goes wrong, it'll only make it more memorable. The choir looks divine, by the way. Those velvet tops and scarves are inspired.'

Sallie followed Holly's gaze. The choir stood in a neat arc near the front, pages of music ready, and a gentle buzz of conversation rippled around. 'They do look lovely,' Sallie admitted. 'It was Juliette's idea with the tartan scarves, actually. She's become a bit of a stylist.'

'Well, she's not wrong.' Xian nodded approvingly as she sipped from her silver hip flask. 'And look at those lanterns down the aisle. You know, it's like a fairy tale in here. I'm in my element.'

For a moment, Sallie let herself take it in because, for sure, it *was* special. The Christmas twinkling, the scent of pine, the guests coming in and taking their seats. The glass roof above reflecting the lights, and beyond it, snow falling thick and dense, blanketing the world of Pretty Beach in white.

'It's still coming down fast and heavy. I can't quite believe it.' Holly peered up through the glass. 'If it keeps going like this, half the town will end up sleeping here tonight. We'll be snowed in.'

Sallie cringed. 'Don't even joke! At least we've got enough Christmas cinnamon buns to keep everyone fed for a week.'

'And mulled wine,' Xian added as she sloshed a nip from her hip flask into her mouth. 'If people get snowed in, no one will mind. It's so beautiful, Sal. You should be proud.'

'Thank you, ladies. I'm grateful for all your help. Right, get yourself settled. Not long until showtime.'

Holly squeezed Sallie's arm. 'You've done it. Whatever happens now, it will be magical.'

As candlelight flickered against the glass, snowflakes floated down in lazy spirals outside, and the choir waited, Sallie prayed everything would go to plan. Looking around at the glint of the lanterns, the sparkle of the tree, and the hum of people finding their seats, she nodded. There really was little more she could do to make it go off without a hitch, other than pray.

In no time at all, The Orangery was packed to capacity. Locals in gorgeous Christmas colours filled every seat, clutching programmes and the choir, all dressed in matching black velvet tops and tartan scarves, stood at the front ready to go. Lucian's cameras were positioned strategically, red lights blinking and already running to catch footage beforehand. Christmas fairy lights twinkled overhead, candles flickered on every surface, and a heady mixed scent of pine and cinnamon filled the air.

Sallie stepped to the front of The Orangery to the left of the tree, glanced at Ben with a flick of her eyes, and prayed that she didn't sound as nervous as she felt. 'Good evening. Welcome to The Orangery for our Pretty Beach Carol Service. Thank you so much for coming! Some of you had to arrive on foot for this, some of you marched cinnamon buns through snow, and some cleared snow from the roof. I am *very* grateful that everyone is here in one piece. Whether you are watching from across the seas or tuning in from nearby, enjoy. Pretty Beach wishes you peace and warmth and a very Merry Christmas.'

The organist gave a discreet thumbs-up, Lucian lifted his index finger, and the red light by the main camera lens winked. Sallie gave the tiniest nod back to Lucian, the first chord rose and filled the sparkling glass building. With the place filling with the sound of the choir, Sallie looked up at the ceiling Ben had strung with lights and garlands and prayed that the weather and the wires would hold. She could but wait and see. As she moved near the back to watch it all unfold, she smiled. Nina caught her eye from three rows back, lifted a hand and mouthed, "You've got this," and the knot in Sallie's chest eased by a thread.

Ben appeared beside her, slipped his hand into hers and whispered. 'You did it. Everyone is in place and it looks magical. I'm *so* proud of you, Sals. You really do know how to pull something off. It's been worth all the work just to be part of this.'

Sallie squeezed his fingers. 'It does look amazing, I have to admit. I'm not counting my chickens yet, but yes, I think I met the brief fairly well…'

'Just a bit! We're nearly there. Not long and we'll be over the finish line. I love you for working so hard.'

'Right back at you. I love you and Loulou and Pretty Beach.'

10

Sallie watched a long stream of words going up the comment window on the side of the channel livestreaming the carol service to the world. The little strip of digital space felt as if it had a life of its own as messages from all over the planet gushed about the event. In a way, the continuously looping comments felt the same as what was going on in Sallie's head.

Despite feeling frazzled and still overseeing the smooth running of the event, Sallie was right in the middle of what was actually a pinch-me moment as she stood and watched the choir do their thing from the back of the room. She'd one hundred per cent built the space around her on a wing, a big mortgage payment and a prayer, and it was paying back its dividends and then some. She'd started her business from scratch, by the skin of her teeth, and crawled her way up step by step, day by day, to a business that was both sustainable and doing well. There'd been many moments of stress, long nights on laptops and early mornings in the cold when, to be quite frank, she'd really thought about throwing the towel in. Now, however, she was so very glad she'd stayed the course. Her independence and worth were more important than the chucking in of towels, and she'd soldiered on through all sorts of shenanigans and dogged hard work left, right and centre. She'd made both The Orangery and her business a success and was as pleased as punch as it all looked back at her.

Dressed the part, as she stood in her very own orangery with carols going on around her and snow falling outside, witnessing the result of her graft, Sallie felt more than grateful. Musing and pondering as she listened to the choir, she let herself relax a little bit, her shoulders dropped, and her frayed nerves eased. It was funny, really, from the outside, she was in no doubt that it all looked very easy to the casual onlooker. Most probably, people thought that she was lucky, that things had been given to her on a plate, that she hadn't had to hustle for it. There she was, lucky duck Sallie Broadchurch, dweller in Pretty Beach, wife to a family of wealth, her own business, the sweetest of babies. Anyone who didn't have a clue what she'd been through and how she'd worked day and night to get her life back might have thought she'd had it easy. How wrong they would have been. Sallie had not been handed anything on a plate. There was a severe lack of silver spoons in her world. She'd made her own luck happen right from the word go.

Pondering how different her past was from her present and that, in actual fact, she was living the dream, Sallie exhaled. Very happy that everything was going swimmingly as the carol service got into full swing, she started to feel tight coils of stress in her head begin to unwind. The choir sang to their hearts' content, Lucian's crew were on fire, and so far, there had not been any hiccups. Every detail, down to the last tealight, had been thought about, and therefore, it was no surprise that it was going well.

Just as she was thinking about having a glass of bubbles to toast the success of the event, a strange popping sound came from her far right, then a flash, followed by a blinking, swiftly succeeded by a bang. Suddenly, the power went out, some of the fairy lights died, the livestream flickered, and the wind whipped around outside. A collective gasping and shuffling sound went through the air, the choir faltered, their voices trailing off uncertainly for a second and Sallie's heart stopped as she stood frozen, not sure what to do. First, she panicked, then event planner mode kicked in, and she automatically looked down at her laptop. So far, so good where that was concerned. Lucian's stream wasn't running off the Wi-Fi; from experience, he'd not wanted to chance it. Closing her eyes as The Orangery sparkled with only the lanterns and battery lights, Sallie was stunned into inaction for a quick minute as she tried to decide what to do. She swore as Ben approached. 'What the heck are we going to do?'

Lucian was up and at the back of The Orangery and by Sallie's side as quick as a flash, his face a picture. Suntanned Pete wasn't far behind him. Lucian shook his head. 'Okay. Good job we're prepared. We've rehearsed for this. The feed is fine, the batteries have kicked in, and there is just about enough light.'

Sallie squinted at the choir, who'd moved onto another carol without a blip. 'Right, yes, the choir seems okay. We're good for another few minutes at least.'

'Are we going to kick the generator in?' Pete asked.

Neither Sallie nor Lucian wanted the generator on. It had been brought in by Pete as a last-minute backup plan because of the weather. Lucian shook his head. 'It will ruin it. The noise is horrid.' Narrowing his eyes, he looked around. 'Technically, nothing has changed. It's just that we all know we have no power and it is a fair bit darker.'

'You're not wrong, it's very dark.' Pete agreed.

Sallie nodded. '*Too* dark.'

Lucian sighed and swore. 'Time for plan C to kick into action.'

'Which is?'

'Haven't the foggiest.'

Sallie was tempted by the generator option, but the noise would ruin the whole thing. They'd find another way. The calm, the carols, and the ambience mattered more than the generator. It had only been brought in for dire emergencies and they weren't there quite yet.

A message flashed on her watch from Nina. *Don't panic. It's still beautiful in the dark.*

Sallie exhaled, tried to remain in control and closed her eyes for a second as Ben turned towards the tree. 'How about we get everyone to put their phone torches on and hold them up? It might actually look amazing.'

Lucian raised his eyebrows. 'Now there's an idea.'

'We'd have to whisper to someone to put the word around without it showing up on the screen.'

'Doable.'

Lucian leaned in close to Sallie. 'Right. I'll go to the back and start it quietly. You two sidle up the aisles and spread the word from there.'

Sallie nodded, heart thudding. Ben disappeared to the left, weaving through the rows as she moved to the right, smiling as if everything was perfectly under control. The choir, still singing beautifully, took the cues right away. Sallie smiled and whispered to Holly. 'We need to get everyone to turn their phones on. It's looking dark on the livestream. Pass it along. We're crossing our fingers that the power comes back on shortly.'

Holly blinked, then nodded, lifted her phone and tapped to turn her torch on. The person beside her did the same. Gradually, a wave of little circles of white light began to appear all around The Orangery. Slowly, even more magic made itself known in Pretty Beach.

Lucian turned back from the far end, caught Sallie's eye and gave her a thumbs up. In less than a minute, the whole place was lit by tiny beams bouncing off the glass walls. Soft, silvery, and absolutely dreamlike, it dropped the wow factor on The Orangery in one fell swoop.

'Well, would you look at that,' Ben said under his breath.

Sallie swallowed hard, half in relief, half in disbelief. 'It's better than before.'

Lucian grinned and looked at his iPad. 'The messages are going nuts!'

The choir carried on and the comment window on the livestream began to zoom upwards like crazy.

This is beautiful.
Pretty Beach knows how to do it.
This is Christmas in a nutshell.

Sallie stood still for a moment, taking it in. The phone lights shimmered across every face, snowflakes drifted past the glass, and the tree twinkled. 'It's actually breathtaking! We certainly didn't have this in the meeting notes.'

'Plan C worked,' Lucian whispered.

Sallie smiled. 'You can say that again.'

~

Sallie continued to operate in planner mode as a gust of wind shook the windowpanes, the snow swirled, and thick, dense snowflakes floated down sideways. From where she stood, she could just make out the outline of the outside Christmas tree through the whiteness, its few battery-powered fairy lights glowing, its star on the top catching the light. For sure, everything looked magical and they'd got past the initial fallout unscathed, but there was no power, which meant no heat, no warmth and upcoming problems left, right and centre.

Scanning the space, she crossed her fingers, her brain jumping ahead to the heating. She'd done enough events in the winter to know that it was crucial that the old glass building did not get cold. Hurrying over to Suntanned Pete, who was checking pipes near the back, she whispered. 'The heating's gone, hasn't it?'

Pete looked up and made a face. Astonishingly, despite the snow, he appeared as if he'd just eased himself off a sunbed in Magaluf. 'Yeah, I'm just having a feel. The system has gone off with the rest of it.'

Sallie bit the inside of her cheek and frowned. 'Brilliant. How cold are we talking before everyone starts noticing? It's freezing out there.'

Pete glanced around, assessing. 'We'll be fine for a bit. The woodburner's still going strong over there. I'll load it up further. We should be fine. There are a lot of us in here to keep it warm for a good while yet. You've got more experience in this old place than me. I don't suppose it takes too long for the temperature to plummet.'

'You're not wrong.' Sallie followed his gaze to the corner, where the huge old cast-iron burner glowed a deep orange behind its glass door. 'It's probably enough to hold it.' She looked outside. 'But it's coming down so fast, it's freezing, and at the end of the day, we're in a building made of glass.'

'I think it'll be fine.'

Sallie looked up at the ceiling for a second and then in the direction of the kitchen. 'At least we have gas for the mulled wine, so that's okay, and it will still be served hot.'

'Once the carols finish, serve it straight away, get everyone's hands around a cup and get that down 'em to warm the cockles...'

'Yep.'

Pete rolled his eyes. 'Nothing like mulled wine and a power cut to keep the festive spirit up. We'll just have to roll with it.'

Letting out a shaky laugh, Sallie tried to remain calm as outside, the snow continued to fall. Inside, The Orangery sparkled, and the choir sang despite what was occurring behind the scenes. Looking over to the woodburner, she nodded. 'Yes, right, okay. We'll make it work. We have to.'

11

An hour or so later, and despite all that had occurred, the event had gone well. The actual service itself had finished, and the live streaming had ceased, although the cameras were still rolling for additional social media content. Just as there had been about ten minutes until the end and the choir had been building up to their last few crescendo numbers, the electricity had spluttered, the lights had come back on, and the heating had cranked back to life. Talk about Sallie being flooded with relief. When the power had been restored, she'd nearly done a happy dance right there in full in front of everyone, including the cameras.

Mostly, when the power had been cut and disaster had loomed, Sallie had been concerned about the locals who'd turned up in their droves in support. The livestream, the podcast and the socials were all well and good, of course, but it was the true blue locals she'd been concerned about. She'd operated from day one in Pretty Beach on goodwill and word-of-mouth recommendations, and the bread and butter of her business were the locals and their backing. Not stupid enough to ever dabble with the inner workings of the town, the success of the event for those who'd trudged through the snow had been Sallie's front and centre right from the word go. In Pretty Beach, locals could, would and *did* make or break a business as quick as a flash. Sallie Broadchurch was well aware of that and never ever wanted to mess with it.

With the carol service having wrapped up, guests stood around with mulled wine, chatting full of the Christmas spirit, and it appeared that the locals were loving it. Sallie, however, was still very much in work mode. On the outside, she radiated calm and elegance, as if she was just like everyone else, standing around chatting over a cinnamon bun and a drink. Inside, her brain juggled balls in the air as she directed the catering and slowly started to tick the final boxes of a job well done.

Ben had gone home with baby Loulou, and the remaining locals were having lots of mulled wine and making the most of it. Taking a glass herself, she sipped as she spoke to Pete.

'So, that went well, didn't it?' Pete smiled. 'Being prepared saved the day. What a turn up for the books. All those meetings we had…'

'Yes, thank goodness. All our hard work and plans paid off in the end. Despite the hiccup with the power, it was great.' Sallie let out a little whoosh of air. 'I have to say I don't want to go through that power outage drama again.'

Pete peered at the window. 'We wanted snow and boy did we get it.'

'I prayed for it one night. I don't think I expected to have my prayers met with quite as much of the white stuff.'

'Tell me about it. I couldn't believe it this morning.'

'I know.'

Just as they were chatting, beside them, Xian went to step to her left to move out of the way of a member of staff with a tray of mulled wine. Then, as if time stopped, she wobbled, slid, hesitated with her hands out by her sides and then slowly collapsed onto the floor in a heap. Panic ensued as one of Pretty Beach's locals went down.

Sallie froze for half a second, glass halfway to her lips as what had just happened failed to register for a moment. Then the noise around her shifted as people began to react; a sharp scrape of chairs, a gasp from someone near the tree, and then, as the staff member with the mulled wine blinked and lost her footing, the sound of the tray hitting the floor cut through the air.

'Oh my goodness!' Sallie's instincts kicked in, and taking a few steps across the tiled floor, she crouched down next to Xian, whose Christmas jumper still twinkled. Pete did the same, and Holly, Xian's daughter, arrived on the scene like a shot.

'Mum!' Holly dropped to her knees.

Xian lay sprawled on her side, head turned slightly, eyes closed, hair spread across the tiles. The tray of mulled wine had rolled to a stop nearby, and the air smelt of red wine, cloves and cinnamon. The girl who'd dropped the tray was frantically picking up pieces of dried orange while another was collecting glass and scraping debris up with a dustpan and brush.

Sallie looked at Holly. 'Has this happened before?'

'No, no, never. I don't think so.' Holly's voice was shaking. 'Never.'

Pete loosened Xian's scarf and checked her wrist. 'She's breathing fine. Pulse is good. She just went out cold.'

'We need to get her head up a bit.' Sallie glanced around, someone handed her a folded coat, and she slid it carefully under Xian's head.

'Give her some space,' Juliette called out to the crowd. A few people shifted back, murmuring, hands clutching half-empty glasses.

'Mum, can you hear me?' Holly brushed Xian's hair away from her face.

Xian stirred, eyelids fluttering.

Relief washed through Sallie. 'Stay still. You've had a bit of a turn.'

Xian blinked, eyes glassy for a moment before she groaned softly and fully opened her eyes. Frowning, she shook her head. 'What are you all doing? Get away with you! I just went a bit dizzy. I tripped over that chair leg…'

Holly clutched Xian's hand. 'Mum, take it easy. You fainted.'

'I did not faint! I just fell over. What are you all looking at?'

Sallie exhaled. 'You gave us all a fright there.'

Xian did not look best pleased and with a frown on her face, she tried to sit up. 'Honestly, I'm fine. Off you all trot.'

'Whoa, hold on.' Pete put his arm around Xian's back.

Lucian appeared, headset still around his neck. 'Right, let's all take a second, shall we?'

'She's fine. She just had a bit of a funny turn, that's all. Everyone's okay.'

Pete helped Xian into a nearby chair, and someone appeared with a glass of water and a cinnamon bun.

'I didn't have lunch,' Xian admitted, looking sheepish.

Holly tutted. 'You've been lugging back your Special Drink all day, Mum! I told you to go easy on it.'

'I do that *every* day.' Xian deadpanned.

Pete blew out a long stream of air. 'Fair.'

Xian smiled. 'I'm fine, I just went a bit giddy and lost my footing. There's nothing to see here.'

Lucian clapped his hands. 'Thank God for that! No more dramas, please. We've hit our quota for the evening.'

A ripple of laughter went around the room, and just like that, the tension lifted. Someone restarted a playlist, a carol hummed softly through the speakers, and as Holly fussed over Xian, Sallie let out a sigh and swallowed. Hopefully, that was the last of the drama for the year.

12

Pretty Beach, being what it was, didn't take long to start talking about what had occurred at the carol service. Of course, locals were much more interested in what had happened to Xian than the snow, the power cut or how the livestream had gone. By breakfast the next morning, everyone from the people in the post office to the bookshop had heard a version of what had taken place. Some said Xian had fainted from the heat, which was most definitely not true because it had been far from warm. Others swore she'd been out cold for ten minutes and that an ambulance had come, lights flashing. None of it was accurate, of course, but everyone assumed that it had something to do with Xian's very own Special Drink. Sallie had more or less come to the conclusion that Xian's little spot of dizziness was, in actual fact, due to Xian being half cut.

Sallie pushed open the door to the bakery, the little bell above jingled softly, and Christmas carols carried through the air. Baby Loulou was fast asleep in the pram, cheeks pink from the cold, as was Sallie's nose. The smell of warm bread and cinnamon hit Sallie instantly, as she took a deep breath and closed the door behind her. From the moment she'd first arrived in Pretty Beach, she'd always loved the smell of the bakery and the sound of its coffee machine hissing, and nothing had even remotely changed. The bakery always somehow instantly calmed, which was never a bad thing.

'Morning, Sal,' Holly called from behind the counter. Despite the usual diamonds at her ears, it had to be said that Holly looked tired, worn out and drawn.

'Morning.' Sallie rolled the pram beside the window. 'Gosh, are you okay? You look shattered! How's your mum?'

Holly hesitated. 'She's still a bit shaky, but she won't admit it. We've told her it's exhaustion. The woman never sits still! She's either trading her shares, working too many hours here, sorting out our properties or playing bridge. I told her she can't keep on doing it, but you know what she's like. She's been burning the candle at both ends for years. What with that and her Special Drink, and we all know what that does, what occurred last night was bound to happen. She's fuelled by that drink, and yesterday she'd hardly had anything to eat. If you ask me, she'd had one too many, but I'm no doctor. She's not getting any younger.'

Sallie nodded. 'I did think she looked done in last night when I first saw her, but I didn't think much more about it because I was flitting around in organisation mode. I should have checked in on her.'

'No, no, it's fine. She *was* running around all day before the service and trying to do too much.' Holly sighed. 'She didn't eat, barely sat down, then got herself in a flap about some deal in New York she'd missed. Something about the stock exchange and how much money she could have made if she'd been online.'

Sallie smiled. 'That sounds about right. How does she even know about that stuff?'

'I have *no* idea. She's always been into it. She thrives on it.' Holly gestured for Sallie to wheel the pram around the back. 'Time for a cup of tea?'

'Yes, of course. I'd love one.'

'Come on, come out here, it's much quieter out the back.'

Sallie followed Holly around the counter and bumped the pram down a step and through to a back room, where the air was warm and filled with the smell of cinnamon, butter and pastry. After pouring two mugs of tea, Holly put them down on a beautiful, old stripped pine table. 'Honestly, Sal, I don't know what to do with her. She's getting worse, not better. It's as if the internet has fuelled her to do more. She never stops. Even after last night, she was trying to get up at five to go on that trading app thing. I was a flat no. I'm not having it. It will be me who has to pick up the pieces if she falls again. Do you know what I mean?'

Sallie nodded. 'She's built it all from nothing. I know what that feels like. It's the same as me. It's hard to let go when it's your name over the door, as it were. It's almost like a drug.'

Holly nodded. 'Yeah, but it's starting to take a toll. Her blood pressure's all over the place. She's supposed to rest, but that's not exactly her strong suit. She's off floor duty in the shop for a week. I'm taking her shifts and I don't want to see her anywhere near an iPad or a mixing bowl until after the New Year.'

As if she'd heard everything, Xian appeared. Holly was instantly on her feet. 'Mum! You should be resting.'

Xian, in a Christmas jumper covered in snowmen, rolled her eyes as if nothing had happened. 'Resting? I've been sitting around all morning doing sweet nothing at all! I am bored out of my brain. I needed to stretch my legs. I can't be doing with sitting around twiddling my thumbs. The world doesn't stop turning, does it?'

Sallie stood and smiled. 'You gave us all a fright last night.'

'So I hear, but it was nothing.' Xian lowered herself down. 'I'm mortified. Imagine collapsing in front of the whole town. I just overdid it a bit yesterday. Because of that New York trade, I completely forgot about lunch. That was why I went a bit dizzy. It was nothing.'

Sallie nodded, not really believing Xian. She more favoured the fact that Xian had lugged so much Special Drink back that she'd been tipsy. 'People were so worried. You're basically Pretty Beach royalty. You faint and it's headline news. My phone was pinging for ages last night and this morning. I had one of the queens of Pretty Beach fainting on my turf.'

Xian groaned and covered her face with one hand. 'I popped down to the shop this morning and someone asked if I'd had a "turn of the heart". I said it was more likely a turn of my Special Drink.'

Sallie laughed. 'Pretty Beach is buzzing with theories. Someone told me you were rushed to hospital in an ambulance, and I'm like, no, that didn't happen, I was right beside you.'

Xian gave a wave of dismissal with her hand. 'Oh, for heaven's sake! No one ever just stumbles anymore, do they? It's all drama this, drama that.'

Holly nodded. 'Well, to be fair, you did faceplant next to a tray of mulled wine.'

'Adds a bit of flair.' Sallie chuckled.

'Honestly, I'm fine. I just need to take it easy and eat properly. I'll admit I've been overdoing it. You know what it's like this time of year anyway, and there's so much going on in the stock market at the moment.'

'I'm hearing you.' Sallie nodded. 'We're all guilty of it at this time of year. I can only say that I'm glad last night is over.'

Xian looked over at Loulou, still sound asleep in her pram. 'I bet you are. Look at her. Doesn't she make you forget all the chaos for a second?'

Sallie smiled down at her daughter. 'She does. Although she was up in the night, so don't let those angelic cheeks fool you. She took ages to settle.'

'You make it look easy.'

'Pah, I don't think so! It's not, but I wouldn't swap it for the world. Besides, we women of Pretty Beach have a habit of getting through things the hard way.'

'Ain't that the truth?' Xian poured amber liquid from her hip flask into her tea. 'Maybe I'll take tomorrow off.'

Holly corrected. 'No maybe about it. You're not lifting a finger.'

Xian gave her daughter a mock glare but didn't argue.

Sallie stood up and straightened her jacket. 'Right, I'd best be off. If you need anything, just shout. I'll leave you to it.' She looked pointedly at Xian. 'Get some rest, and for goodness' sake, no trading marathons. Surely you don't need to make any more money?'

'We'll see,' Xian muttered. 'For the record, I always need to make more money.'

13

Sallie's old house felt as if it had settled as the dead of a snowy Christmas night had laid itself thickly over the whole of Strawberry Hill. Her beautifully dressed tree sat in the corner of the sitting room by the window, throwing light across the hallway floor, snow continued to flutter from the sky, and fairy lights twinkled from just about everywhere. The windy, blustery, blizzard-y feel had dropped and instead, an eerie silence from the deep insulation of the covering of snow had descended upon the whole of Pretty Beach.

Sallie stood at the kitchen worktop next to the Aga with a stack of lists and cross-referenced them against a Google Doc from Lucian. Once satisfied as if she were mentally ticking off achievements that included surviving a power cut, she slid the bundles of notes together and tucked them into the pocket on the cover of her iPad. For the first time since the carol service, she allowed herself to breathe. It was as if she'd been running on empty for weeks and now, finally, here she was ready to recharge. Even though she'd physically stopped running around organising the event, her brain was finding it a challenge to stop galloping.

Putting the kettle under the tap, she waited for it to fill, lifted the Aga cover and plopped the kettle on the plate. Looking at the baby monitor camera, she could see Loulou fast asleep upstairs with both fists up near her cheeks and enjoying much-needed sleep.

Ben came downstairs from the shower, kissed Sallie on the cheek, and she nodded in the direction of the Aga. 'Tea?'

'Please. Thank goodness it's toasty in here. It's getting colder out there now that the weather has really set in. Got to love that Aga.'

'I know.' Sallie pointed out to the back garden. 'It's still falling, but the wind has died down.' She wrapped both hands around the mug and felt heat move through her fingers and into her chest.

'What's happening on the socials regarding the carol service?'

'Lots of great feedback and loads of new followers.'

'It went well.'

'Everyone is saying it was magical. It did turn out quite magical in the end.'

'It really did. Not being funny, but I didn't expect anything less.' Ben stated.

'I did *not* enjoy the power cut. I smiled and told people it was fine, but I wasn't fine inside. When the lights came back I felt sick, not happy. Sick with relief.' Sallie put her mug down and looked at the floor. 'I know I do this to myself. I know I set the bar high, but I can't help it. Yeah, so thank goodness we pulled it off in the end.'

'You do do it to yourself, Sal, and it's not over yet. You still have two Christmas weddings to do. I did say no to you doing them.'

'I know. Why did you let me say yes?'

Ben laughed. 'You think I had a say? You told me your revenue needed it.'

Sallie groaned. 'I feel as if I am failing at all of it. I need to be good at The Orangery events, and I want to be good at being a mum, and the truth is that some days I'm neither. I cried in the larder the other day, Ben! I mean, really? Who even am I?'

'It's just Christmas stress. Roll on Boxing Day. You are putting your feet up, and for the record, you are not failing at anything.'

'It feels like it. I wanted Loulou so much and sometimes I think I'm letting her down.'

'Don't be ridiculous!'

'She does her thing with cheeks like peaches and I sometimes feel mean because I find myself counting the minutes until her next nap because I am so tired my eyes burn. I look at you and I love you and then I snap sometimes.'

'You don't have to earn any of this by being perfect. You have me. I am here. Loulou has two parents. The Orangery has a team. You don't have to hold all of it on your own shoulders because you once learned that the only way to be safe was to do everything yourself.'

'I don't even know how *not* to do everything myself.'

Ben smiled. 'Well, the good news is that there aren't many seaplanes taking off while everywhere is covered in snow. I will write a list, and you will cross things off, and we will count down to having some time off. You can give me the exact jobs you hate. I will do those. If there are too many, we will ask for help. It's as simple as that.'

'I wish it were.' Sallie exhaled and closed her eyes for a second. 'I promised myself I would do this year with grace. I do not think I have nailed grace or anything like it.'

'Pah to grace! Life is messy, and small business is not for the weak. You just need a last push to get through these next two events.'

'Yup. One last push and I'm done.'

Later that night, once the house was quiet and the fairy lights glowed in the darkened kitchen, Sallie opened her laptop. Slowly, she began to cross things off on all sorts of lists and realised that the schedule she'd been clinging to for dear life was nearly coming to an end. As the fact that she was nearing the finish line of her work commitments for the year and a Christmas break with nothing planned other than whether or not to have another mince pie percolated through her brain, she closed her eyes in pleasure for a second. She'd only gone and done it. She'd nailed her best carol service yet and she was on the home run. It couldn't have come sooner.

14

With one of the two weddings under her belt, Sallie was on her way to the bakery with Loulou in the pram. The sky had dawned a watery blue, the pavements were clear of snow, but the roofs and tops of buildings were still covered in the white stuff. Christmas lights looped from window to window, little trees stood outside houses and everyone was getting ready for Christmas Eve.

Sallie pushed the pram along the lane and nodded to the florist who had propped the door open as she put small Christmas trees in pots out onto a trestle table. A woman outside the post office said hello and mentioned that the phone torch part of the carol service had been the most romantic thing she'd seen for a long time. Sallie had chuckled to herself and not let on that the torch episode had most definitely not been part of the plan. No one needed to know the fine detail.

Going around to the rear of the shops, Sallie pushed the chair up the path of the bakery's backyard and made her way into the kitchen area at the back, where Holly, Xian, one of their staff, Chloe, and Juliette were meeting for coffee and mince pies. Xian, with gold earphones around her neck and a headset with a flesh-coloured microphone across her cheek, was studying an iPad in one hand and the Financial Times in the other. Sitting on a chair with a cup and a saucer on the table and a blanket over her knees, she had a smug look about her person. 'You're looking very pleased with yourself.' Sallie laughed as she got Loulou out of the pram.

Xian nodded very slowly, made a funny face and swished the newspaper back and forth. 'I've just had the best deal I've had for a long time.'

'I wish I could say the same. I thought you weren't allowed to be working?'

'She's not.' Holly rolled her eyes. 'Tea?' Holly asked without waiting for an answer and began to pour tea from a pot into a mug. 'You look more yourself today.'

'I slept all night and I only have one more event to go.'

'Good. You deserve a day without running around like a headless chicken.'

'I think I do.'

Holly lifted her phone. 'Have you seen Lucian's behind-the-scenes edit?'

Sallie braced. 'I haven't. Do I need to sit down?'

'You'll like it.'

Xian peered over her iPad. 'The comments had me in tears. People need nice things and you made a very nice thing happen. We like you.'

Sallie tapped her phone and opened a behind-the-scenes video Lucian had uploaded. The footage opened on the glass roof of The Orangey as snowflakes hit, then swept down to a lantern glow and faces turned up to the ceiling lit by small squares of light. A cut to Ben by the door with a storm lantern made her smile. Lucian's voice, in his podcast tone, narrated. 'Pretty Beach. It's magical here.'

'He's right, you know.' Juliette broke a mince pie in half. 'Pretty Beach does Christmas properly.'

'It does.'

'I still can't believe how many people turned up in that weather.'

'The choir was amazing,' Chloe added. 'I'm still humming the tune of "Hark the Herald".'

Holly laughed. 'You'll get another chance at church. We're all going, aren't we?'

Xian folded the newspaper. 'I wouldn't miss it for the world. Front pew for me, same as always.'

Juliette brushed crumbs from her lap and looked at Sallie. 'Are you still coming or are you off duty now the big night's over?'

Sallie smiled, adjusting Loulou on her lap. 'Of course! I think we've earned a few church carols and candlelight. Loulou deserves to see it all from the front row.'

Holly nodded. 'It'll be packed. The reserved seating went ages ago. Word is, the choir's doing a new arrangement of "Silent Night" with the children showcasing a sweet part at the end.'

'That's my cue to cry.' Juliette sipped her tea and popped a piece of mince pie in her mouth.

'Mine too,' Sallie admitted.

Holly smiled. 'You can let someone else handle the cables and the cameras, Sal.'

Sallie sighed. The thought of sitting in the pews, not having to think about anything, and just listening felt amazing. 'For the first time in months, I'll be officially off duty.'

Loulou let out a small sigh as they chatted about Christmas Eve. For once, Sallie didn't make a list in her head, think about what she had to do and wonder whether or not she would fail. Instead, she simply listened and smiled as the conversation rolled over her. It felt lovely to be part of the small-town community. More importantly, it felt fabulous not to have anything to do. Long may it last.

15

On Christmas Eve, the afternoon slid quickly into dusk. One minute day, the next evening. The light sat low over Pretty Beach's rows of pastel cottages and the colour of the harbour had turned to pewter. Special edition Christmas bunting that had survived the snow fluttered from lamppost to lamppost, and as Sallie approached the church, she smiled as it sparkled in its Christmas coat of festive decorations. Like everything else in the town, it had gone all out for the festivities. Outside, a cluster of locals held lanterns and directed people to their seats. Suntanned Pete stood with a clipboard in front of him, and Nel, the bus driver, dressed in a red Christmas suit, bossed people around.

Sallie pushed the pram up the path and smiled as she got to Pete. 'Evening, Pete. What a lovely night for it. Merry Christmas.'

'Merry Christmas. Ahh, yes, Sallie, Ben, plus two and Loulou. You have a space reserved up the front. You're right behind the queens and Juliette is to your left. Row two, right-hand side. Where's Ben?'

Sallie gestured behind her. 'He's arriving with his parents. I walked the long way around so I could have a look at the harbour and get Loulou some fresh air.'

'Yep, right, so they'll be along in a minute. Right you are. Enjoy.'

Sallie took her gloves and hat off as she walked into the church and felt more than grateful that she had nothing to organise, do, think about, plan or say. No heating to check, no candles to turn on, no people to worry about and no food to sort. And breathe. The church glowed in the way only an old English church can at Christmas; all stone walls catching the light from hundreds of candles set in sconces and on window ledges, the air carrying a mix of incense, pine, chilly winter air and brass polish. Above the pews, garlands of holly and ivy dotted with red berries trailed across the beams as an enormous Christmas tree by the altar shimmered in white lights. Someone had tucked a small gold angel among the branches halfway up, slightly wonky, and it made Sallie smile.

As hats came off, scarves were unwound, and coats rustled as people shuffled along pews, the vicar, in a red stole embroidered with gold thread, stood by the font chatting. Holly waved to everyone from her seat near the front. Xian, beside her with a fur-lined cape that sparkled each time she moved, had replaced her regular oversized headphones with a small, discrete pair. Juliette and her husband Luke were side by side in the second pew, their hands linked, and the choir to the left at the front was ready to go.

Sallie eased herself into her seat and adjusted Loulou on her lap, and five or so minutes later, Ben slid into the pew beside her, brushing snow from his coat, his parents following behind. Giving Sallie's hand a squeeze, he nodded at Loulou. 'All good with her?'

'She's taking it all in.'

Just after Nina had arrived and got settled, the organ swelled, everyone stood, and once the first carol was sung, the vicar's voice carried through a tiny microphone attached to her front. 'Welcome, everyone, to our Christmas Eve service here in Pretty Beach. Whether you've come from near or far, we're glad you're with us tonight. Merry Christmas.'

Candles flickered, and with Loulou on her lap as the second carol began, Sallie felt a prick of tears at the side of her eyes as she followed the words on the carol sheet. For a moment, the whole world seemed to pause as she thought about the previous few weeks and shook her head. The snowstorm, her internal panicking, the carol service that had almost gone to pieces, and had somehow become more perfect because of it. She thought about The Orangery lit by phone torches, Xian's funny turn, Lucian's theatrics, Pete's calm practicality, and Ben's love. How much she loved her home on Strawberry Hill went through her head, and as Loulou wriggled, she realised how she adored being a mum. Ben squeezed her hand as she glanced around at the people she loved. Ben, his parents, and her friends scattered through the pews looked back at her. Her life in Pretty Beach wasn't perfect, not by a long shot, but it wasn't far off it and it was mostly certainly hers.

Pressing tiny little kisses to Loulou's forehead, Sallie wiped a tear away as she thought how lucky she was to be in Pretty Beach. She'd landed in the place down on her luck, not much hope in her head, ready for the next blow. The little town by the sea, however, had taken her under its wing. Now it was home.

16

In tartan Christmas pyjamas and matching slippers, Sallie padded quietly down the stairs and walked into the kitchen. Flicking on the tree lights, she inhaled the fir scent and sighed. Quite frankly, she was glad to see the back of the previous few weeks. Let the eating, drinking and mince pies begin. After putting water into the pot along with a couple of spoons of special Fortnum's Christmas blend, she took cinnamon buns from the fridge, laid them out on a tray and stuck the tray in the Aga to warm. After checking on the turkey, she mentally ticked off everything on her to-do list and realised that most of her boxes were checked. With Ben's family and Nina for dinner, she'd had to be organised and had planned right up until she'd gone to sleep the night before.

Ben pushed open the door and kissed her. 'Merry Christmas.'

'Merry Christmas to you.'

Ben jerked his thumb upwards. 'She went back down. We have a window.'

Sallie giggled. 'An actual gift from someone looking down on us.'

'Yup.'

After laying out a tray with the teapot and bits, Sallie plonked down on the sofa in front of the fire as Ben piled kindling logs onto the last embers in the woodburner. Turning the tree lights on with the app on her phone, she sat and watched as they twinkled, so very pleased it was Christmas Day. Reaching for one of the cinnamon buns, she sighed. 'What a lovely start to our day. Peace, quiet and a cup of tea.'

'Ahh, for sure it's not going to be this quiet later.'

Sallie shook her head. 'We've gone and got ourselves a houseful somehow.'

Ben poked at the fire until it gave a crackle. 'How did we manage that?'

'God knows.'

'The turkey is my domain this year.'

Sallie raised an eyebrow. 'You're claiming the bird, now I've done all the hard work?'

Ben was adamant. 'Absolutely, that's my point. From now on, *you* are doing nothing. I know you've seen to all the preparation, but I'm taking the reins from here as discussed.'

'Good. I've already parboiled the potatoes, pigs in blankets are prepped and ready, and the stuffing's in the fridge waiting to go in. The gravy's mostly made, the cranberry sauce is done, and the sprouts are trimmed. Basically, it's foolproof for anyone to step in. You're welcome.'

'Foolproof and my cooking do not go together. Dangerous words.' Ben took a bite of a bun.

Sallie chuckled. 'You can't scare me. I've been through worse this month. I've survived Lucian, a blizzard, a livestream broadcast around the world, two Christmas weddings, a power cut, Loulou and her teeth, and Xian fainting at The Orangery. Christmas lunch is going to be a breeze compared to that lot.'

Ben leaned back, looking smug. 'I'm timing everything. You

just have to sit there and sip bubbles, play with Loulou, and wear something sparkly.'

'Oh, I intend to, don't you worry about that. I'll supervise with a glass of champagne in hand, and Loulou and I will offer encouraging noises from the sofa.'

Ben smiled. 'It'll all be fine. Nina will bring that huge salad she always does, my mum will pretend not to scoff too many roasties, and by the time we get to pudding, everyone will be too full to care. My dad will shove After Eights into his mouth on repeat...'

Sallie laughed. 'That sounds exactly like the kind of Christmas I like. Predictable chaos, lots of food, and everyone talking over each other.'

Ben stretched his legs towards the fire. 'And afterwards, we'll collapse on the sofa, eat too many Quality Streets, and I'll fall asleep through some rubbish film. Sound about right to you?'

Sallie smiled into her mug of tea. 'I think we should also partake in a Christmas walk to the pub.'

'Nice.'

'For now, let's just enjoy the quiet bit before the madness begins.'

Ben nodded. 'Merry Christmas. We made it and I love you.'

Sallie watched the fire flicker, feeling utterly content. 'Merry Christmas, Mr Chalmers. Nice spending the festive season with you.' Looking into the fire, she let out a long, contented, very happy sigh. She was in Pretty Beach with Ben and Loulou at Christmas. That, really, was all that mattered in her life.

17

A few days later, it was that funny limbo-esque time between Christmas and New Year. The weather had not let up, and it had continued to snow in Pretty Beach. Now that her events were over, Sallie lapped up the white stuff. Little sparkles of white clung to the tops of hedges, the rooftops of houses sparkled, and the coastal path along the cliffs was topped with a layer of white. Pretty Beach had exhaled after Christmas Day had done its thing. Fairy lights still looped from window to window, lovely wreaths sat on doors, but the main rush of the festivities had eased into a lovely post-Christmas calm. To Sallie, it felt as if the whole town had slipped into that slow pocket of time after Christmas where the world went quiet and everyone ate leftover turkey and rummaged around in the bottom of tins looking for the strawberry creams.

With Pretty Beach Radio playing from the windowsill and Ben having braved the cold to take Loulou out for a walk, Sallie was pottering around the kitchen, doing what she loved: getting the table ready for a cosy, informal, post-Christmas get together. Laid-back, snug, no fuss and most definitely not an event that would be livestreamed around the world, she'd been looking forward to it a lot. There wasn't a run sheet, a real lack of a sponsor and certainly not a camera in sight. Just Sallie in her kitchen, lovely food, gorgeous drinks and the people who had rolled the carol service over the line invited over as a way to say thank you.

Spraying and wiping the large ten-seater table, Sallie smiled as she pottered. The fir and eucalyptus garland with its white lights, cream pillar candles, and tiny gold baubles still looked as lovely as it had on day one. Sliding a tray from the Aga and putting it on a thick wooden board, she inhaled the smell of pastry and smiled at the pie she'd made. Turkey, leek, and ham, it had been part of her Christmases for as long as she could remember. Made with the leftovers from the big day, she always looked forward to making it as the soft, quiet days at the end of the year did their thing. Every year, she'd roll out the pastry, crimp the edges, brush on a layer of egg and cut a little fir tree in the centre for the vent. As she checked, it sent out a ribbon of scented steam that smelt of leeks and ham and looked like love and home.

She heard Ben come back in with the pram. He poked his head around the door. 'Do you need any help with anything?'

'Nope, I've done it all. The pie is ready, I'll just keep it warm now until we're ready to eat. The panettone bread and butter pudding is done. I'll pop that in nearer the time.'

'Drinks?'

'Can you just get some more beers from the garage?'

Ben nodded and inhaled. 'It smells so good in here.'

Sallie chuckled. 'After that huge Christmas meal, I never thought I'd be hungry again, but this is going to do the trick. I mean, who could not love potatoes roasted in turkey dripping? I don't even want to think about the calories involved.'

Ben patted his non-existent tummy and very present six-pack. 'I'll need a cleanse in February.'

Sallie shook her head and made a face. 'You're on your own

there. You won't be finding me doing a cleanse in any shape or form.'

A couple of hours later, Sallie smiled as she heard Suntanned Pete coming through the front door. Arriving in the kitchen with a crate balanced on one hip, an orange face and pink board shorts topped with a smart shirt and boots, he saluted. 'I've got mince pies, wine, Locals Only growler which will knock your socks off and white crackers which I thought would fit your aesthetic.' He looked around at the decorations. 'And I was correct on that score.'

'Merry Christmas, Pete! You look well.'

Pete inhaled. 'It smells marvellous in here. I thought I'd eaten enough already. What's cooking?'

'A lovely Christmas pie, panettone bread and butter pudding and roasties with turkey dripping. I aim to please. I love this time of year. I have been pottering around to my heart's content all day.'

Pete slid the growler and a bottle of wine across the table, 'I can handle some of that. I like the idea of Christmas pie. I think I'm going to need to start a fitness regime come February.'

'You can join Ben in a cleanse. He just mentioned it. I won't be partaking.' Just as Sallie was putting the wine in the fridge, Juliette and Luke came in. Juliette's coat looked as if it had stepped out of a Christmas film, pale pink and soft, with a hood edged in fur. 'Hey.' Sallie kissed Juliette and Luke.

'Hiya. How was your Christmas?'

'Really lovely, thanks.'

Juliette placed a large glass footed bowl covered in a tea towel on the table. 'This is the trifle. I think it will need to go in the fridge. It might have to be my last trifle of the season. I haven't stopped eating for days.'

'Same here. Ooh, I love your trifle. How are you?'

'I'm good, a bit tired, actually. Lots of babies decided to appear this year. I feel like I haven't slept for two days, but yes, overall I'm fine.'

Luke laughed. 'I feel the same.'

Xian shuffled in behind them, wearing a green scarf covered in reindeer, gold headphones and thick slouchy cream socks tucked into open-toed sliders. Holly, beside her with cheeks pink from the cold and eyes bright, beamed. 'We have cinnamon buns and all sorts. Gosh, it smells *fabulous* in here. You are a woman of many skills.'

Chuckling, Xian waved her hand. 'I've made extra of my Special Drink especially for the occasion.' Xian appeared to be deadly serious. 'Even though Holly has put me on rations. I am basically living under house arrest, but I thought you lot might like some.'

Holly tutted. 'You'll thank me later. We don't want you fainting again, though I am not sure that was a fainting episode, more a tipsy episode.'

Suntanned Pete nodded. 'I have to agree.'

~

An hour or so later, everyone was sitting around the table. Nina had arrived with her daughter Tilly, Sallie's neighbour Lottie and her husband and one of her sons had turned up, Lucian had descended, and Ben's parents were sitting fussing over Loulou. The pie, potatoes, a huge salad and bubble and squeak were in the middle of the table. Sallie stood up. 'Right. I just wanted to say thank you all for helping with the carol service. I couldn't have done it without you. The whole shebang went off well in the end, but for a moment or two there, I thought we were in trouble. Yes, so just thanks very much.' She gestured along the centre of the table. 'This is to show my appreciation.'

Juliette smiled. 'It really was a great night in the end.'

'It was! I actually loved the moment when the lights went out,' Lottie nodded. 'Everything stopped and then started again, but slower. I just adored it.'

Sallie made a face. 'Really? God, my heart went in my mouth when that happened.'

Juliette shook her head and widened her eyes. 'The phone torches ended up being spectacular, especially when I watched the wrap-up on Lucian's extra video. That first dot of light and then all the others. It looked as if we'd planned it, which we very much didn't. Best laid plans and all that.'

'The choir not missing a beat was the bit I thought was great.' Ben smiled. 'They were like professionals or very good amateurs.'

'The mulled wine after the power came back and everyone cheering at a hot drink as if it were a miracle,' Holly said. 'I liked that a lot.'

Pete chuckled. 'I just loved watching it all come together in the midst of the crisis. Funny the things you notice when you stand with your back to a door and pretend you are security.'

Xian cackled and held her glass up. 'Mine has to be having rather too much of my Special Drink.'

Lucian rolled his eyes. 'Darling, *that* made it.'

Sallie looked around as everyone chatted. She really did feel *very* fortunate. She'd gone from arriving in the little town by the sea with a broken heart, a whole lot of sadness and a suitcase or two. Now, here she was surrounded by community, friendship and love. Pretty Beach had seen her well. One thing she knew without a shadow of a doubt: she was there to stay.

POLLY BOOKS

(Reading Order available at authorpollybabbington.com)

Love from Pretty Beach
All My Love from Pretty Beach
Much Love from Pretty Beach

The Bookshop Pretty Beach
Whispers at The Bookshop Pretty Beach
Always at The Bookshop Pretty Beach

A Cottage in Lovely Bay
Sunshine in Lovely Bay
Forever in Lovely Bay

One Nice Day in Lovely Bay
One Sweet Day in Lovely Bay
One Perfect Day in Lovely Bay

The Summer Hotel Lovely Bay
Wildflowers at The Summer Hotel Lovely Bay

Seashells at The Summer Hotel Lovely Bay

The Old Ticket Office Darling Island
Secrets at The Old Ticket Office Darling Island
Surprises at The Old Ticket Office Darling Island

Spring in the Pretty Beach Hills
Summer in the Pretty Beach Hills

The Pretty Beach Thing
The Pretty Beach Way
The Pretty Beach Life

Something About Darling Island
Just About Darling Island
All About Christmas on Darling Island

The Coastguard's House Darling Island
Summer on Darling Island
Bliss on Darling Island

The Boat House Pretty Beach
Summer Weddings at Pretty Beach
Winter at Pretty Beach

A Pretty Beach Christmas
A Pretty Beach Dream
A Pretty Beach Wish

Secret Evenings in Pretty Beach
Secret Places in Pretty Beach
Secret Days in Pretty Beach

Lovely Little Things in Pretty Beach

Beautiful Little Things in Pretty Beach
Darling Little Things

The Old Sugar Wharf Pretty Beach
Love at the Old Sugar Wharf Pretty Beach
Snow Days at the Old Sugar Wharf Pretty Beach

Pretty Beach Posies
Pretty Beach Blooms
Pretty Beach Petals

Printed in Dunstable, United Kingdom

74902044R00057